And slowly—ever so slowly—he touched them to hers. Maggie wanted him more than she had ever wanted anything. Her face burned with the heat of her own temptation, but she pulled away. She was too old to be taken in by sexy words and wet kisses.

Jake leaned against the wall and grinned longingly at her. "You're tough, aren't you?"

"Not nearly as tough as you might think."

"Then you want me, too?"

"I'm a normal, functioning woman. And I'm probably no more immune to that special Jake Abel charm than any other woman is. I'm just smarter."

His grin grew more amused. "I didn't know there was a special Jake Abel charm."

"Yes, you did," she said. "And you know how to use it. But that's okay. I'm no teenage virgin. I can handle it."

"You may think you can," he said. "But I'm not going to sleep until I get you in my bed."

Dear Reader,

No doubt you've noticed the different look to your American Romance novels. Now you're about to discover what's new between the covers.

Come with us and sail the high seas with a swashbuckling modern-day pirate...ride off into the sunset on the back of a motorcycle with a dark and dangerous man...lasso a cowboy Casanova and brand him your own. You can do it all with the *new* American Romance!

In this book, and every book each month, you'll fall in love with our bold American heroes, the sexiest men in the world, as they take you on adventures that make their dreams—and yours—come true.

Enjoy the new American Romance—because love has never been so exciting!

Sincerely,

Debra Matteucci
Senior Editor & Editorial Coordinator
Harlequin Books
300 East 42nd St., 6th floor
New York, NY 10017

TRACY HUGHES

SAND MAN

Harlequin Books

TORONTO • NEW YORK • LONDON
AMSTERDAM • PARIS • SYDNEY • HAMBURG
STOCKHOLM • ATHENS • TOKYO • MILAN
MADRID • WARSAW • BUDAPEST • AUCKLAND

For Ellis,
for all the special moments
that make lifetime memories.

Published September 1992

ISBN 0-373-16455-6

SAND MAN

Chapter One

If the student body had looked like this when I was eighteen, I'd have a college degree now. Maggie Conrad grinned as she peered from the second-story window of the Fine Arts Building to the campus courtyard below, where students scurried back and forth, completing the lengthy process of registration. Gorgeous men with overdeveloped pecs and biceps and muscular thighs darting around under the warm Florida sun in T-shirts and gym shorts were quite an advertisement for an institute of higher education. But that wasn't why she'd decided to go back to school.

At forty, she had another chance to pursue her dream of a college degree, and she had earned it. Right now, however, that task seemed minute compared to figuring out how to get from the Fine Arts Building to the Math Building with only fifteen minutes between classes, but if she had to don roller skates and a jet pack, she'd make it. Already she'd figured out that it wasn't the smartest who survived in college, but the fastest.

Mentally, she measured the distance between point A and point B and decided to give it a trial run. She looked at her watch and, poised like a marathon runner out for the gold, waited for the second hand to reach the twelve. The second the imaginary starting pistol fired in her head, she lit out down the hall, racking her brain to remember whether the stairwell was on the left or the right. *The left,* she thought before reaching the turn. Speeding up, she soared around the corner and checked her watch to see how she was doing.

She had scarcely gone three feet when she realized she had taken the wrong turn and was in the exhibit hall, but as she turned to correct the error, her foot snagged a strategically placed Oriental rug—a death trap to those who had the bad taste to sprint through a museum—and she tripped. A marble stand holding a statue was the only thing close enough to grab on to, so she reached out and grasped it, pulling it down with her.

It was like a slow-motion nightmare, worse than the one in which she went to school without her clothes, as the statue hurled through the air. Mortified, she tried to catch it before it hit the ground, but it slipped through her fingers, crashed to the floor and shattered into a million pieces.

"Oh, my God!" she shouted, as if she'd single-handedly destroyed Michelangelo's *David.* What would they do to her? Throw her out of college before she'd even gotten started? Would they arrest her? Would she have to pay, or did they have insurance for this kind of thing? Frantic, she tried to gather up the broken pieces, as if she could puzzle it back together before anyone noticed.

"Way to go, kiddo," a voice said above her. Maggie jerked her face up to see a man who, she was certain, had stepped out of a Marlboro/Hanes underwear/

Coppertone ad. "I spent two whole hours on that masterpiece."

Maggie came to her feet and with a distraught, apologetic look on her face, handed him the pieces she had picked up. He took them with a wry grin.

"Am I supposed to do something with these?" he asked.

Maggie covered her face with a shaky hand, then swept her fingers back through her tousled red hair. "I can't believe this," she said. "My first day on campus and I break a priceless piece of sculpture. And I don't even have the grace to do it in private where I could sweep up the pieces and throw them away before anyone notices. No, I have to do it right in front of the artist himself."

The man chuckled, and Maggie noticed the deep dimples in the sides of his cheeks and the beginnings of laugh lines around his eyes. Suddenly she wondered if this was, indeed, a nightmare or just a dream that was getting more interesting by the moment. "I wouldn't exactly call this 'priceless,'" he said. "It's really just the university's token exhibit of pop art. Truth is, I have twenty more just like it at home."

Maggie found that his laughter was contagious, and finally letting go of her humiliation, she took a deep breath and held out a hand. "I'm really sorry. I'm Maggie Conrad. I'm new here, and I guess I took a wrong turn."

"Hi, Maggie." He took her hand and held it in both of his. "I'm Jake Abel. And if it's any consolation, I'm *not* new here, but I still take wrong turns. You'll get used to being lost."

Maggie's heart fluttered at the grin in his eyes, and she told herself that she hadn't felt a flutter like that since she was fourteen and ran into Elvis in a hotel elevator. Jake, however, looked better in jeans than Elvis had.

"So... have you found your way to The Grill yet?" he asked.

"The grill?"

"The campus hangout. You can't call yourself a bona fide student until you've hung out in The Grill."

She grinned. "Oh, then I'll have to get right over there."

"There's no time to waste," he teased. "As a matter of fact, I was just heading over there myself. Could I buy you a cup of coffee?"

Maggie gaped at him, and before following her instinct to decline, told herself that she had led a decent, productive, selfless life and—forget coffee—she deserved a whole night with this man. Then she told herself that he was young enough to be her son...almost. Actually, he looked to be in his mid-twenties—maybe even older, if she stretched her imagination. She cleared her throat and withdrew her hand. "I should be buying you coffee. As a matter of fact, I should pay you for that sculpture."

"All right," he said, assessing the damage in his hand. "You owe me one more smile like the one you gave me just a minute ago, a few minutes of your company and a cup of coffee. How's that?"

Unbidden, Maggie's smile flowered across her face. "You're on," she said.

He stepped over to the garbage can in the corner of the exhibit hall and dumped the pieces of his sculpture into it. Then dusting his hands off, he turned around. "Now..."

Like Rhett Butler come to escort Scarlett to the front porch, Jake held out a tanned arm for Maggie to slip her hand through. She took his arm and was delighted with the feel of his biceps beneath the light cotton. His confident smile smoothed away her worries about his age, and she told herself that a cup of coffee never hurt anyone. In fact, it could do her a heck of a lot of good. Besides, she needed a friend on campus, and she couldn't have found a better candidate if she'd created him herself.

If she could only keep her mind off his body and those killer eyes and that hair that looked as though it had been specially favored by the sun. If she could only remember that she was a mature woman seeking an education, not a roll in the hay.

But as they walked and he pointed out the buildings of the campus to her, teasing and chiding and charming as they went, she told herself that rolling in the hay had great therapeutic value. And she was about due for some good, fun therapy!

WONDER WHAT SHE'D BE LIKE *in bed*. The thought sang through Jake's head like the chorus to an overplayed song as he smiled at Maggie across the table in The Grill. Would she love with the same reckless abandon he saw in her eyes? She was older, he thought, quite a bit older, but that was really more apparent in her voice and her wit than it was in her face or body.

And what a body, Jake thought, trying to keep his mind on what she was saying.

"I just can't help envying all these students who look like they know where they're going. They all look so young, but they have a knowledgeable air that makes them look so sophisticated."

"Right," he said sardonically, "if you define *so-phisticated* as a bunch of clones with permed, brittle, tangled hair and expensive clothes that look like they've been dragged out of the bottom of a Goodwill bin."

Maggie laughed and Jake felt the sound somewhere in his chest, like a piece of sunshine melting away years of frost. "When I graduated from high school," she said, "the look was long, straight hair—the straighter the better—tight body suits and bell-bottom jeans with peace insignias embroidered on the seat. And that was the men *and* women. Of course, I was attracted to the type of man who had hair longer than my own, rarely shaved and preferred carrying a guitar to a load of textbooks." She paused and sipped her coffee, then laughed and shook her head. "If only I had known then what I know now."

"What would you do differently?" Jake asked, fascinated.

"Everything," she said. "I'd be a psychologist now, I'd never look at price tags and I'd eat out whenever I wanted. Oh, and I'd have some hunk for my husband who delighted in every move I made and would never, ever consider leaving me for another woman." Her smile faded, and she traced the rim of her cup with a finger. "Funny thing is, in my day there didn't seem to be any men like that. I guess that's why I wound up divorced."

"In your day?" he asked with a chuckle.

Embarrassed, she covered her face. "Uh-oh. Did I really say that?"

"You sure did," he admitted, setting his chin on his hand, "but it sounded so out of character to me that I'm gonna pretend you didn't."

"Out of character?" she asked. "How do you know what my character is?"

"Hey, I'm a terrific judge of character." He watched her with amusement, and his voice dropped to a rumble. "And you're definitely not the kind of woman who should use the phrase 'in my day.'" He reached across the table and took her hand. "*This* is your day, darlin'. Don't you forget it."

The easy way he touched her and called her "darlin'" made Maggie blush unexpectedly, and suddenly she felt like an innocent in the presence of an experienced older man. His big hand enveloped hers with sizzling warmth, and she had to remind herself that *she* was the older one. A lot older. Too much older.

As if he noted her embarrassment, he let go of her hand and picked up her class schedule. "So tell me about the problems you're having with this educational obstacle course. It must be pretty bad to send you rocketing through the museum."

She laughed. "I just don't know how they expect me to make it from one building to another across campus in fifteen minutes or less." She realized she was babbling, but if she didn't babble, she'd have to concentrate on the way her hand had felt buried in his, and on the scrutiny of those sexy, inescapable eyes. "The thing is, it's impossible to get a parking place, so it isn't feasible to take my car from one class to the next. But how am I supposed to get there on time if they're two miles apart?"

"Not really two miles," he said, pointing at the map of the campus. "In fact, this isn't that hard. All you do is take the back door of the Fine Arts Building, cut through the Music Hall, slip through the Liberal Arts Building and there you are."

"Can you do that?" she asked, frowning at him.

Jake chuckled, his baritone voice vibrating through her chest. "Darlin', you can do whatever you want. They don't have hall monitors here."

She hid her self-conscious grin behind her coffee cup. "I guess you can tell it's been a long time since I've been in school. And never in college. I've been working as a secretary for the last—" He waited for her to confess how long so he could tell her it didn't matter, but she amended her thought and said, "Well, the last few years."

"Yeah? So how are you gonna manage that and school, too?"

"I've cut my hours back to part-time," she said. "I've saved for a long time for this." Jake watched her content, self-satisfied smile as she leaned back and looked around her, and for a moment, she looked eighteen and totally innocent to the new world she had embarked upon. He decided that he liked that look a lot. It was foreign to him. Most women weren't that innocent—at least not the ones he knew. That look was also very sexy, and Jake realized it was the first time in a long time that his libido had kicked in for a woman who wasn't even wearing a bikini. But unable to be anything but completely honest with himself, he admitted that there was nothing he'd like more than to see her in one.

"So...are you working on an art degree?" she asked, focusing those effervescent green eyes on him again.

He nodded. "Yeah. It's my second time around. I quit college a year before getting my degree last time. I decided there were more important things to do."

"Really? Like what?"

His irreverent grin shot into her again. "Like sand and sun and women."

An incredulous look transformed her face. "You quit college for that?"

He shrugged. "Seemed like a good idea at the time."

Her melodic laughter was addictive, and it drew out a need he rarely felt—a need to express what he really meant. Somehow it mattered that she understand him. "I decided I was a pop artist with great potential, not to mention a philosopher. So I set out to redefine the term 'beach bum' as someone who knew how to live on the sand and still make a living. And I did. I have a pretty good little beach business during the summer. They call me the Sand Man. People from all over the world have my sculptures on their mantels, and some of them even believe they're worth something. Little do they know that I turn them out by the dozens...."

"So what made you come back to school?" Maggie asked. "I mean, you sound like you're doing well."

His face grew more serious, and he looked down at his cup. "I turned thirty last year," he said, "and decided there had to be more to life." His grin inched across his face again, and he added, "I was really only doing it so I could be on the beach all the time, and once you've seen two thousand bikini-clad women you've seen them all. Besides, there isn't much future in sand. There was something to *The Three Little Pigs*, you know."

"So you think the Big Bad Wolf is going to huff and puff and blow it all in someday?"

"No," he said, "more like a redhead is going to come speeding around a corner and *knock* it all in."

She winced. "Ooh. I'm really sorry."

"Nothing lost," he said, chuckling. "That's the point. I want to do something more important. I really want to be a serious sculptor, and believe it or not, I'd like to teach. I'll graduate after this semester, and then I plan to go for my master's."

She gazed at him for a long moment, her smile laced with a touch of poignancy. "I admire you," she said. "Anyone who can make it for years on his talent and wits...well, that's really special. Most people can't take those kinds of risks."

"It wasn't a risk," he said. "It was really just plain cowardice. Now, what you're doing—coming back to school after being out for years—that's what I call a noble risk."

Her eyes lit up again, and she looked around her. "It's a wonderful risk. A well-earned risk. I've dreamed about it for years, and I never really thought I could make it happen. But here I am."

"Here you are," he said, that grin cutting through her awe and shooting into the most vulnerable part of her heart. "And here I am. I should probably warn you, Maggie. I'm a great believer in fate. And I can't help thinking that fate brought you barreling around that corner today."

"And why would fate do that?" she asked, knowing she was being coy.

"Who knows?" he asked, taking her hand again. "But I intend to find out."

As Maggie pondered his intention with her heart pounding and her mind mesmerized by the euphoria of unexpected attraction, she followed him to the cash register, where he paid for their coffee, in spite of her protest that she had agreed to pay. Then she thought about it more as he escorted her back to the Fine Arts

Building, where her car was parked. Before saying goodbye, he took her hand, kissed it, and said, "I'm really glad you ran into my sculpture today, Maggie Conrad."

She hoped her smile didn't reveal the fluttering in her heart. "I'm sort of glad I did too, Jake Abel. And thanks for the coffee and the tips about getting to class."

"No problem," he said. "When can I see you again? I was thinking of dinner at this new little French restaurant I found the other day."

She withdrew her hand and gaped up at him. "What?"

"Maggie, I told you that fate had something to do with our meeting, and I make it a habit never to ignore fate. Now, when can I see you again?"

For a second she was speechless, for it was the last way she'd expected the afternoon to end. "Why would you want to?" she asked. "I'm—I'm a little older than you—"

"I like older women," he said. "Unless you're embarrassed yourself...."

"No, not at all!" She swallowed and told herself that she shouldn't be concerned that he could have his pick of the university sex kittens. He had asked *her*, and that was all that mattered. Besides, she was starting a new life and she deserved a little fun. There was a time to analyze, and a time to enjoy; a time to ask questions, and a time to be content with simple feelings.

"All right," she said finally. "I'd love to have dinner with you."

The moment Maggie was in her car, she mentally kicked herself for agreeing to go on the date. What could she have been thinking? Was she crazy?

The only reason he'd asked her was that he hadn't seen her clearly in the light. The Fine Arts Building had been relatively dark, and The Grill needed to replace a few bulbs. It had been overcast outside, so he hadn't seen all the little wrinkles on her face or the gray hairs on her crown.

And what would she wear on a date with a man like Jake Abel—a *thirty*-year-old beach bum. Jeans? A dress? A bikini? The dilemma made her cringe, and she felt her spirits sinking. She was an idiot, that was all. She should have given him a false address. She should have told him she was engaged. She should have run like hell the first time he smiled at her.

How could she kid herself into thinking her saggy, high-mileage body could attract a man who'd seen the best buns on the Florida coast? It was hopeless.

And yet she couldn't help feeling a little exhilarated that he'd asked in the first place. He must have seen *something* in her, and hey, she had to admit, she wasn't all *that* bad. Not for an old broad.

Laughter edged up in her throat as she pulled into her driveway, and she decided to treat this like the greatest hoax ever pulled on a man by a woman. She would act as if she were the most desirable woman in town. Age difference? Was there an age difference? She would have fun for the first time in years and, by golly, if he didn't come away feeling bowled over, he'd at least realize he'd been out with someone different.

That, she supposed, was enough for her. One date with Jake Abel would be enough to launch her like a cannonball into her first week at college. After all, she was a single woman finally living alone without the limitations of motherhood. She would take advantage of her new freedom and show them all what lay beneath the Maggie Conrad she'd been for years. She'd—

Maggie stopped cold as she saw the suitcases and boxes piled on the back steps, and her fluttering heart sank like a wounded bird.

"Hi, ya, Grandma," Maggie's son-in-law shouted from behind the screen door. "Guess who's moving in!"

Chapter Two

Maggie tried to tell herself that she was still dreaming, but once again the unfolding event constituted nightmare status. "I'm not a grandmother yet, Steve," she bit out, trying to ignore the other part of what he'd said. The part about moving in. The part that explained all these boxes.

"Hi, Mom." Her daughter opened the screen door to let Maggie into her own home, and bracing herself, she stepped inside.

"What's going on? What are all these boxes for?"

April rubbed her seven-month-pregnant belly, the way she always did when her mother started to lecture her, and Maggie knew it was a reminder of her "delicate condition," something April had milked for everything it was worth since the first day she'd found out she was pregnant. The fact that she hadn't been married at the time hadn't seemed to bother her, for Steve had married her instantly and moved her into his parents' home. It had taken Maggie this long to get used to the fact that her daughter had left her comfortable nest for a man who wore an earring and had soapsuds for brains, but now that she had, she wasn't ready for the whole situation to be reversed.

"Mom, we had a little problem with Steve's parents. They don't understand anything, and they're always on Steve's back, and—"

Maggie swung around to her son-in-law as a thought popped into her mind. "Why aren't you at work, Steve?"

He shot his wife a doleful look, then settled his eyes on his tennis shoes. "I sort of...got the afternoon off."

"Oh, no!" Maggie said, slamming her purse down on the table. "You got fired again!"

"Not fired," Steve said indignantly. "I quit this time."

Maggie scraped out a chair at the table and plopped into it. "How could you quit? You needed that job. You have a baby on the way! It couldn't have been that hard! All you had to do was wash cars!"

"Yeah, well, how would you like standing around in the heat washing cars all day? I deserve better."

Maggie felt a headache coming on and began to massage her temples. "Steve, we all deserve better. But life doesn't give us what we deserve. When are you going to figure that out?"

"He's looking for a management position, Mom," April said in his defense. "He can do a lot more for our baby if he has a good job."

"Yeah, and I can't go for decent interviews if I'm in a pair of shorts, soaking wet all day."

"So you just quit? What did your parents say?"

Again, Steve and April exchanged looks.

"Uh...well, they—"

"Mom, they're not like you. They could never understand."

"Like me?" Maggie asked with a mirthless laugh. "You think I do understand? What did they say?"

"Well, their rear ends were a little chapped about it," Steve said.

"And they . . . sort of . . ."

Maggie turned to April, waiting for the punch line. "They sort of what, April?"

"They threw us out," Steve blurted out.

"Threw you out? As in, no place to live? Are you telling me you don't have a job *or* a place to live?"

April cradled her stomach with her hands, but this time the gesture didn't have the impact that it usually had on Maggie. "Mom, we knew you wouldn't turn us away."

Maggie dropped her face into the heap of her arms and shook her head viciously. "No! I can't afford to support all of you. I just cut my hours back to part-time so I could go to school. I just dropped a wad into tuition, and I'll be studying all the time." She jerked her head up and gaped at them both. "And what about the baby?"

"Well, it's coming whether anybody likes it or not," April said. Tears came to her eyes, and she went to stand beside her husband, as if together they could fight these evil, unreasonable forces around them. "Mom, I know you weren't thrilled when I got pregnant, but Steve could have run out on me. He didn't. We're married now, and we love each other, and we're excited about the baby, but we need a little help. . . ."

She'd heard it all before, but somehow, each time it was repeated to her like some majestic Shakespearean speech, Maggie found herself capitulating. The last time, it had cost her three hundred dollars. The time before that, she had loaned them her car and had to hoof herself to work for a week. Mentally she pictured herself sawing off an arm and handing it to her daughter. *Here, will this help? Sure you can have a leg, too. Need anything else?*

Instantly, she felt guilty. She knew she was being selfish. April was her daughter, and she had no one else. It should be Maggie's privilege to help her child when she was in trouble. And if trouble wasn't being pregnant, homeless and married to an unemployed idiot, then she didn't know what was.

Trying to boost herself up, Maggie took a deep breath. "All right, you can stay here for a while. I had converted April's room in to a study, but we can bring the bed back in." She gave Steve a long-suffering look. "Steve, do you promise me you'll find a job?"

"Of course, Mags. I don't want to be a vagrant. I've got a lot of potential."

She gave him a look that conveyed her doubt. "Potential doesn't pay the bills, sweetheart."

"I know. It'll be all right. You'll see."

"And you need your own place, so you won't have to keep jumping around from parent to parent. Your baby'll need some stability."

"It's on my list of goals," Steve said. "Honest."

"And one more thing—" she stood up and faced him, her expression deadly "—if you ever call me Grandma again before that baby comes along, I'll hire a hit man to kill you in your sleep. Got that?"

Steve grinned. "A little touchy about that, aren't you?"

"Call it whatever you want. Just don't call me Grandma until I really am one."

"And then?" he asked.

"And then there won't be anything I can do about it."

His voice was edged with laughter as he gave her a noncommittal shrug. "Whatever."

Maggie stared at him with eyes that lacked motherly compassion. "The bed's in the storage room. You might as well get started putting it together."

"Thanks, Mom." April planted a kiss on her face. "You won't regret it. You'll hardly even know we're here."

Cheerfully, Steve and April disappeared for the time being, leaving Maggie to contemplate the fact that the couple were about as quiet and discreet as Tasmanian devils, and she most certainly would know they were there every minute of the day.

She remembered her loneliness, months ago, when April had first married and moved in with Steve and his parents. April would have been the one to start college this year, but the baby had changed all of her goals. In the midst of her empty-nest loneliness, Maggie had set some goals for herself.

It seemed that the moment she allowed herself to re-structure her dream and her plans for going after it, her loneliness evaporated like a cloud on a sunny day, and she had begun to see her aloneness as something to be cherished. She had never known what it was to think only of herself. For eighteen years she had centered her life around raising April, and it had been no easy task, since April's father had long ago disappeared and hadn't paid a penny of child support in over fifteen years.

Now she couldn't wait to embark on her new life. But it wasn't going to be exactly the way she had planned it.

Quickly, Maggie tried to think of the changes this new twist would bring about. With April and Steve living with her, she wouldn't be able to practice the art of denial about her age and her impending grand-motherhood. And anyone who came over would have to confront them....

Anyone who came over. Even tonight. Even Jake Abel.

Maggie closed her eyes and told herself that she didn't deserve this nightmare. But what was it she'd told Steve only moments ago? No one really got what they deserved?

Groaning, she again dropped her face into her arms, and told herself that, maybe, she had set her sights too high in deciding to go out with Jake. Maybe it was a stupid mistake. Maybe it wasn't too late to back out gracefully.

She wasn't ready for her daughter to find out that she was going out with a college student, and she es-pecially wasn't ready for Jake to see that she had a grown daughter—a married, pregnant daughter, who wouldn't rest until she'd made Maggie a grand-mother! She'd rather he had time to get used to the first few disappointments—the ones about her sagging body, the gray hairs that he probably couldn't see in the poor lighting today, the wrinkles, the gaping differ-ence in their ages....

Panic overcame her, and jumping up, Maggie grabbed the phone book and began flipping through the *A*'s.

His name jumped out at her, as if it were destiny that she find it. She took the phone, held it against her chest for a moment and closing her eyes, rehearsed what she would say. Something about being sick. A cold—that was it. She'd tell him that she was contagious and didn't want to infect him.

Slowly she punched out the number, waited with breath held and cringed when he answered.

"Hello?"

His voice was as sexy on the phone as it had been in person, and she squeezed her eyes shut and told herself that it wasn't too late. She could hang up and still go through with it.

"Jake?"

"Yeah."

"It's Maggie Conrad. Remember? The redhead who barreled right through your sculpture?"

"The one with the tired feet?"

Maggie frowned. "What do you mean?"

She heard the grin in his voice. "Well, if they aren't tired, they should be, because you've been running through my mind all afternoon."

His vocal smile was contagious and she bit her lip, suddenly unable to remember why she'd called. "You're good, you know that?"

He laughed. "And I didn't even scratch the surface yet. For instance, I was wondering if your eyes are sore."

"My eyes? No, they're fine."

"That's funny. The memory of them has been killing me."

Maggie laughed. "So what have you got there? A book with lines to knock women off their feet?"

"No, darlin'," he said. "I don't need a book. Just a little inspiration."

Again she struggled to remember the reason for the call. "I . . . uh—"

"Only five hours and counting," he cut in. "And then you can put me out of my misery."

"Your misery?"

"Yes. The misery I've been in since you left campus today. Fate's getting real impatient, you know. And I'm a little anxious myself."

That was it, she told herself. She had called to cancel the date. Cursing her restored memory—not to mention her age, her anxieties and her child—she plugged her nose and spoke. "Well, I'm afraid I'm going to have to—" she let her voice trail off, and feigned an Oscar-winning sneeze "—to cancel. I've come down with a cold."

"A cold? You were fine a little while ago."

"I know. It came on suddenly." Again she sneezed, and congratulated herself for making it sound so authentic. She should change her major to theater, she told herself.

"So... you really want to cancel?"

"Well, I don't want to...I just have to. I would hate to make you sick on our first date."

The silent stretch that passed told her that he wasn't happy, and somehow, that gratified her. For a fleeting moment, she wished she had come up with another plan. Meeting him somewhere, for instance. That way he wouldn't have had to meet April and Steve, but she still could have gone out with him.

Unfortunately, she was too much of a coward, and she knew that the real reason she had canceled was the pure, unadulterated terror she felt in her heart. The terror of spending time with a man like Jake Abel, who obviously didn't know what he'd gotten himself into. She didn't want to be around when he was walloped with the realization.

"Well... I can't say I'm not disappointed."

"Me, either," she said.

"And after fate went to all that trouble."

"It probably wasn't really fate," she said. "It was just lousy timing and a Herculean case of clumsiness."

"I like fate better," he said. He was quiet for a moment, just long enough for her to become aware of the pounding in her heart and the turmoil in her nervous system. "Then we can try it again when you feel better?"

Her grin was weaker this time. "Of course. The very minute."

"Well, all right. Pop a couple antihistamines and hurry up and get well."

"Yeah, I will."

She hung up the phone, still smiling.

"Who was that?"

Maggie jumped as though she'd been caught at something and turned around to see April waddling back into the kitchen. "Nobody. A friend. Why do you ask?"

April gave her a strange look. "No reason. Jeez, you're jumpy. I just wanted to tell you that Steve's gonna set up the bed and then we're going out. We have a party to go to tonight. I'm not sure what time we'll be home...."

Maggie's face crashed. "You're going out?"

"Yes. Why?"

Maggie fought the urge to scream that, had she known, she would have left her plans the way they were. Jake would have been coming long after April and Steve left. But it was too late, and it was probably for the best. It was a sign, she decided, that this little fantasy about Jake was just that—a fantasy. It should be nipped in the bud. Maggie was as strong a believer in signs as Jake was in fate, and she followed them whenever she could. They often led her astray and got her lost, but that hadn't stopped her from believing in them.

"Nothing. Never mind," she said absently.

"Jeez, Mom. You sure are acting weird."

"You're telling me," Maggie said, and scuffed to her bedroom, feeling every bit her age for the first time that day.

MAYBE IT ISN'T TOO LATE. Maggie's hope fluttered back to life as she listened to the sound of her car taking Steve and April out of the driveway. Maybe she could call Jake and tell him she was feeling better.

But would that make her seem too anxious? Too unstable? She honestly didn't know, but if there was one thing she had learned over the past few years, it was to take her laughs wherever she could get them and not worry so much about how stupid they made her look. So what if Jake thought she was an idiot? If he did, she'd just make sure she never saw him again. In the scheme of things, what difference did it really make? Ten years from now—when she was fifty and he was forty—she wouldn't even care that he still laughed about that old broad he'd had that mercy date with.

She looked his number up again and taking a deep breath, dialed.

"Hello, this is Jake . . ."

Maggie let out a low moan as that deep voice rumbled from an answering machine.

"I'm not home right now, but if you'll leave your name and number, I'll call you back."

The beep sounded and she dropped the phone into its cradle. Another sign, she told herself, flopping back onto her bed. Some things just weren't meant to be.

Things like forty-year-old women and thirty-year-old men. Things like grandmothers and college students. At this very moment, Jake had probably moved on to plan B and was out with one of those bikini goddesses he fished in from the beach. He'd probably never give her another thought.

The doorbell rang and she rolled over, trying to decide whether to answer it or pretend she wasn't home. It was probably one of Steve's tattooed friends or one of April's airhead cronies come to "party" at the new digs.

The bell rang again and finally Maggie pulled herself up off the bed. She was getting old, she thought miserably. And she didn't feel like putting on a happy face for anyone.

She opened the door and instantly confronted Jake Abel, leaning against the doorjamb with a sexy grin on his face and a brown grocery sack in his hand.

"Jake!"

"Blame it on fate," he said, "but I warned you that I never ignored it. Besides, I felt sorry for you, all sick and everything. And I was disappointed. I don't like disappointment—it makes me kind of impulsive. So I came over to see how you're feeling."

The honest outburst brought a smile to her face, and Maggie bit her bottom lip and tried to forget that she wasn't a seventeen-year-old on her first date with a college senior. Had he been that tall earlier today? Had his shoulders been as broad? Some burning hunger was born in her core, and she told herself this was one of those signs sending her over the side of a cliff. But what the heck, she thought. She had always wanted to learn to fly.

With a reckless smile that belied her sick condition, she said, "Fine...much better, in fact. Come in."

Jake pushed off from the doorjamb and ambled in. "On my way over here, I was thinking of an excuse to come, since I didn't want you to think I was too anxious or anything." That dimple in his left cheek redefined itself, and his eyes twinkled with humor. "And all of a sudden I thought how I hate to be sick and not have the right stuff."

"The right stuff? What do you mean?"

He opened the bag and began withdrawing the contents and handing them to her. "Medicine. So I went to the drugstore and stocked up for you. We have antihistamines, we have decongestants, we have a thermometer, we have aspirin. And...what's this?" He paused and winked as he stuck his hand farther into the bag for the last item. "Oh, look, it's a masterpiece by that famous sculptor Jake Abel. A one-of-its-kind original!"

Maggie let out an uninhibited laugh as he pulled out a sand sculpture exactly like the one she'd broken that day and handed it to her.

"I love it! Can I keep it?"

"Do whatever you want with it, darlin'," he said. "You can smash it or toss it or—"

"How about if I put it on my mantel?" she asked.

"That'll do."

Maggie cleared a place on the mantel and set the sculpture there, then backed up and looked at it. She felt Jake walk up behind her, felt his presence looming over her.

She turned to face him. "Thanks, Jake. All this... you really didn't have to."

"I wanted to. I was really looking forward to our date. Now go take some of it, so you'll feel better, and we can sit around and watch TV or something. Unless you're one of those people who's really grumpy when she's sick, in which case I just remembered somewhere I need to be...."

"No, I'm not grumpy," Maggie said, laughing. "Besides, I've already taken something, and I feel better. We could go out if you want."

"Really?"

"Sure."

Again he gave her that sexy, lopsided grin that she thought needed to be photographed and slapped on the cover of calendars all over the world. "I knew my instincts were right," he said. "They always are."

MOMENTS LATER, Maggie was still contemplating Jake's comment about his instincts, when she realized how he was going to take her on this date. There was no car in the driveway, no van, no cab... only a Harley-Davidson motorcycle with two helmets.

It was *her* instinct that told her to run, but she swallowed back that urge and told herself she was embarking on a new life. She had never ridden on a motorcycle before, and it was time she tried it. And she would lie down and let him ride over her rib cage before she'd let him think she was a boring conservative afraid of taking chances.

Trying not to look as nervous as she felt, she pulled on the helmet, but didn't have a clue how to fasten it. Jake looked down at her, grinned and began hooking the chin strap for her.

"So, have you ever ridden a Harley before?"

"Not lately," she said. "Not since that summer I spent with the Hell's Angels."

"Born to be wild, were you?" he asked, not believing a word. "I can just see you riding behind a big bearded man with three tattoos on each arm—"

"And a bug between every tooth," she added.

When Jake laughed, Maggie felt a warmth shoot through her, as if she'd just taken a belt of hundred-proof whiskey. She suspected he could be just as intoxicating. "You've really never ridden, have you?"

"Never," she said, throwing her leg over the back part of the seat. "But that doesn't mean I haven't always wanted to. No one ever offered before."

"Well, that's a damn shame. All I can say is, it's a good thing I came along."

I was just thinking that myself, Maggie thought as he straddled the Harley and set her hands around his waist... his tight, small waist. But his shoulders were broad and big and made it impossible for her to see around him. Which was just as well, she supposed. Her terror wouldn't be quite as heightened if she couldn't see where they were going.

He started the Harley, the sound loud and aggressive and as intense as the anxiety in her heart. As he pulled out of her driveway, the wind began to whip through her hair and clothes, and Maggie felt herself laughing aloud as she clung tighter to him.

"What's so funny?" he asked over his shoulder.

"Nothing," she cried. "It's just so much fun."

"I told you you were born to be wild," he shouted.

They laughed as he revved the engine and headed toward the beach.

Chapter Three

Jake felt Maggie's arms tighten around him as they reached the beach and began flying across the causeway toward his home. She was so small, he thought, and so happy. He couldn't remember ever being with someone who enjoyed things so much.

"My turn!" she shouted over his shoulder, her voice competing with the wind whistling around his helmet.

"What?"

"My turn," she said again. "I want to drive."

"I thought you said you'd never ridden a bike before."

"I haven't. Now I have to make up for lost time."

Laughing, he pulled over to the side of the road and slid off the bike.

Her eyes were effervescent with excitement as she slid into his spot.

"You're really going to let me?"

"Sure, why not? They're doing great things with skin grafts these days."

"Skin grafts?"

"Yeah. That's what they do for you when you skid across a parking lot at sixty miles an hour on your side."

"Then I'll avoid the parking lots," she said, taking the handles and pretending to drive. "If I think I'm losing control, I'll head for the water."

"Good thinking. Drowning's a much better alternative."

"Besides, you can always reach the handle if I mess up. I wouldn't wrestle you or anything if you thought I was getting us into trouble."

Jake threw his leg over the seat behind her and tested his arms to see if, indeed, they could still reach the handles. Her back was snug against his stomach, and her small hips fit perfectly in the vee of his legs. He reached the handlebars and found his face just above her shoulder, snug against her cheek.

"You're right," he said, his voice a deep rumble against her ear. "This ought to work just fine."

For a moment, he thought he felt a flush of heat sweeping up her cheek, and the realization that he could do that to her sent a wave of excitement through him. He liked the feel of her against him, the thought of their bodies close, the idea of his arms enclosing her.

"So what do I do?" Her voice had dropped an octave, as if his nearness had given birth to a poignant timidity in her.

Jake grinned. "Turning the key would be a good start."

"Then what? I mean, I need to know in advance in case it takes off without my being ready."

"It won't take off until you give it gas," he said. "Right here. Like this."

He turned the handle, demonstrating how it worked, and Maggie tried it herself. "Okay, got it. Now, how about the brakes?"

He showed her how they worked and felt her body tensing as she turned the key and started the engine. "Are you sure you want to do this?"

"Of course, I am," she said. "Now hang on."

Slowly, she revved the engine enough to make the bike roll slightly, and as she got comfortable with the feel, she gave it more gas and they began moving a little faster.

Moments later she was soaring across the causeway, screaming with delight, and Jake admitted he had never had more fun with his motorcycle before.

MAGGIE'S LAUGHTER competed with the noise of the engine droning out across the Gulf, until Jake tightened his arms around her waist and pulled her tighter against him. Suddenly Maggie felt her humor fade and a deep feeling of anticipation edged up inside her.

Was she really sitting here, driving a Harley, with a college student who made her libido go into overdrive? Or was this just one of those mid-life daydreams she'd been warned about?

"You tired of driving?" he asked, his voice a vibration against her ear.

She shivered and thought that she'd rather be on the back now, with her arms wrapped around Jake so that she could bask in the warmth and sensuality of his presence instead of concentrating on keeping them from getting killed. "Yes," she said. "You take over."

She pulled over and let him slide off, then scooted backward, surrendering his seat. Jake grinned at her before he got back on, and leaned down, much too close to her face. "You're a wild woman, you know that?"

"I try," Maggie said, wondering just how "wild" she could be when the situation demanded it. She had never been tested enough to know.

"Let's ride on the sand for a while," he said as he slipped back onto the bike and pulled her arms tightly around him. "See if we can get a little spray going. You aren't afraid of getting wet, are you?"

"No," she said, forgetting the cold she allegedly had. "Let's do it!"

He revved up the engine and pulled out across the sand, went down to the harder sand at the edge of the surf and put the bike into higher gear. They flew over the white tips of the waves, sending a spray several feet into the air. Their laughter lilted and mingled with the wind.

They had gone several miles when a bonfire caught their eye up ahead and a group of young men and women came into sight. A tent with Greek letters on the side loomed behind the bonfire.

"Gamma Phi," Jake shouted over his shoulder. "It's my old fraternity. They must be having a party. Wanna go?"

"Are we allowed?" she asked.

"Sure, we are. Once a Gamma Phi, always a Gamma Phi. I was a real big shot in it my first time around in college."

"Then let's go!"

He slowed their speed and rode precariously across the sand, until they reached the hundred or so people milling around, drinking beer, sitting on blankets, wading in the waves and listening to the loud, blaring sound of rap music.

Maggie pulled off her helmet and shook out her hair, then looked around at the students, most of whom were her daughter's age, doing what she'd heard about for years. "Partying" was what April called it, but somehow, Maggie had pictured something a little more decadent.

Jake took off his helmet and messed up his hair. He took her hand, making Maggie feel instantly like a teenager again, and vaguely, she wondered if forty-year-olds held hands anymore. She wasn't sure because it had been so long since she'd been "attached" to a man. But it didn't matter, she supposed. She liked it. Quite a bit. And she didn't want him to let her go.

Instantly Jake pulled her into the crowd of people he seemed to have known for years, and she watched as the women preened and primped upon seeing him.

"Hi, Jake," one brittle blonde said, rubbing her hand along her bikini-clad hip, though she wore a T-shirt over her top that barely covered her navel.

"Hi, Lori," Jake said. "I'd like you to meet my date, Maggie Conrad."

Maggie extended her hand to shake, but the girl looked slightly taken aback by the gesture. Awkwardly, she shook.

"It's my first frat party," Maggie said. "I'm not sure what goes on at frat parties, but I can't wait to find out."

"Well, not much," the girl said, popping her gum and glancing bewilderedly at Jake, who didn't seem to notice. "People get drunk, mostly, and they just party and dance and ... stuff."

"Come on, Lori. Nobody can dance to that rap trash," Jake said. "Put on some real music."

"That's Hammer," Lori defended.

"I don't care who it is, you can't dance to it. How about some Bonnie Raitt or something?"

"What's the matter?" Lori asked. "You too old for rap? Getting stale?"

As if the comment had been meant to sting her personally, Maggie laughed and took his hand. "Come on, Jake. You can dance to this. It's great. Listen to that beat."

She began to dance, even though she hadn't done it in years and didn't know if she looked perfectly ridiculous. But the intoxication of the night air and the wind and the motorcycle ride had done something to her—set her free in some way—and she found herself without the inhibitions she had normally cloaked herself in. So what if she didn't fit in here? So what if she was with a man ten years younger than she? So what if this party wasn't her usual crowd? She intended to have a good time.

Jake took up the challenge and began to dance with her, until others joined in, and before they knew it, at least two dozen people were dancing to the rap song.

When the song ended, a loud whoop and applause went up around them, and laughing, Jake pulled Maggie against him. Someone tossed them each a cold, wet can of beer, and she popped the top and drank.

"You're a hit," he said, grinning at her over his can. "I know you probably hear this all the time, but you're a fun date."

"Me?" Maggie felt her face flushing again, and she told herself it was caused by the heat of the fire. "No, no one's ever told me that."

"Then you've been dating jerks."

"Or no one. I haven't been getting out a lot lately."

"Well, I intend to change that," he said.

Their smiles locked, and suddenly, Maggie wanted nothing more than to be alone with him, but they were here, surrounded by a hundred partying frat brothers and their dates, not to mention all the others who had crashed the party.

"I probably stand out like a sore thumb here," she said.

He laughed. "Well, you do stand out, but not quite like a sore thumb. More like a rose among weeds."

She looked up at him, her eyes sparkling with the reflection of firelight. "That's really sweet, Jake. But I was referring to my age."

"I was referring to your beauty."

The laughter in her eyes faded, and she felt once again the way she had in high school when a boy said just the right thing and she'd spent the rest of the evening wishing she could stop by a pay phone to call her best friend and tell her all about it. Only now she didn't have a best friend to share the joys of dating with. She'd been alone for too long. She supposed her daughter was the closest person in her life, and April would never understand.

"You're not so bad yourself," Maggie said. "I noticed more than a few girls preening when they saw you walk up. I feel a little overdressed not wearing a bikini."

"I like what you're wearing. Besides, don't you think I've seen enough bikinis for a lifetime?"

"Can you ever see enough?" she teased. Then mocking him, she said, "So many bikinis, so little time."

Jake grinned. "Believe me, it gets old after a while." He feigned seriousness and shrugged. "Sometimes I just sit around wishing a beautiful woman wearing full armour would come into my life."

"Someone who wouldn't wear a bikini if it would save the world?"

"Someone who didn't feel the need to flaunt her flesh to get a man's attention."

"Maybe she knows if she does, he'll run the other way."

Jake pulled her against him and whispered close to her mouth, "I guarantee you if you ever show me your body, I won't run anywhere."

Maggie looked up at him, wet her lips and wondered if he was going to kiss her right here in the middle of the dancers, where everyone could see. Somehow, she didn't mind if he did.

His lips met hers with brash tenderness, and she closed her eyes and slid her arms around him. And suddenly it didn't feel as if they stood in the middle of a hundred other people. Suddenly it felt as if they were alone on the planet, and the rap music, as loud and abrasive as it was, served as an aphrodisiac to their hungry spirits, heightening the mood plaguing each of them.

Jake broke the kiss and looked down at her, and Maggie felt her face reddening again. She was breathless, she thought with embarrassment, and she wondered if he could feel her heart pounding against her breast.

The song was slower now—as slow as a rap song could be—and he didn't let her go, but pulled her into a slow dance that seemed a natural phase to enter from the kiss that had swept her off her feet.

Slowly, she laid her head on his shoulder and followed his lead as the song played and the rapper rapped in a whisper. She saw a few girls clustered in a corner, watching Jake with envy and lust, and she smiled slightly, for it was obvious he wasn't interested in any of them.

But why me? her heart cried out. *Why would he want me?*

She wouldn't think about that tonight; it didn't matter. Tomorrow was a long way away, and she'd wasted too much of her life worrying about tomorrows. Tonight was all that mattered.

Her eyes scanned the crowd a bit further, across the guys who would soon be sick from too much beer, the ones working on seductions of their own, the ones discussing football with buddies while ignoring their dates and the ones being the clowns and the lives of the party.

And suddenly her eyes collided with a pair of eyes staring at her coldly, horridly, through the dancers.

April!

As if she'd been caught out past her curfew, Maggie jumped back and gaped at her daughter.

"April, what are you doing here?"

The words were out of her mouth before she realized it, and at once she wished she had pretended not to know her. Now April would probably call her Mom in front of everybody here, and there would be a terrific, embarrassing scene, and Jake would be humiliated that he was dating the mother of a pregnant woman, and the sky would fall and the earth would swallow her up....

But April didn't call her anything. "What am *I* doing here?" she asked.

Jake looked from one to the other, frowning. "Do you two know each other?"

It had been inevitable, Maggie thought. She had known it was too good to be true. She should have followed her first sign and cowered at home. Next time she would.

But her daughter seemed no more apt to give her identity away than Maggie did herself. Glancing from side to side, lest anyone should be listening, April said, "Uh . . . yes. We had a class together last summer."

As if Maggie would have corrected her immediately, as if she *wanted* the thirty-year-old hunk next to her to know he was dating a grandmother-to-be, April shot her a warning look that admonished Maggie to keep her mouth shut. "Yes," she said. "An aerobics class."

The absurdity of that comment—regarding a woman who, last summer, would have been just a few centimeters smaller in the stomach than she was now—struck Maggie as funny, and she struggled not to laugh.

April's lips grew tighter and more compressed by the moment. "Imagine meeting you here."

"Imagine," Maggie said, grinning now.

Jake nudged her, as if reminding Maggie to introduce him, but some cowardly voice inside kept her from it. Awkward silence stretched like a fog between them.

"Could I speak to you alone for a minute?" April asked suddenly.

Maggie nodded. "Of course. Excuse me, Jake. I'll be right back."

Jake watched, bewildered, as Maggie and April walked far enough away from the party not to be heard.

"Mom, what in the world are you doing?" April whispered furiously. "This is a *college* party!"

"Well, I'm a college student."

"Are you *dating* that guy?" she asked, horrified. "A man half your age?"

"I'm forty, not sixty," Maggie said, insulted. "He is not *half* my age. He asked me out, and I decided to go. I'm having a wonderful time."

April held her face in horror. "I can't believe this. Please, Mom, don't tell anyone you're my mother! Please! I'd be so embarrassed! To be at the same party as my *mother*!"

"Wouldn't it be awful?" Maggie said, deadpan. "I mean, heaven forbid that a mother should ever have a good time. Don't worry, sweetheart, I wouldn't think of humiliating you that way. We're not going to hang around that much longer. I want to get out of here before Steve calls me Grandma."

"I'd die!" April said. "I'd better find him and warn him before he sees you."

"Do that," Maggie said. "Meanwhile, we're leaving."

"No, *we'll* leave."

"No," Maggie said. "They're your friends. I'll leave, and you just have fun. But don't stay out too late. You need your rest when you're this far along. Steve forgets sometimes."

"I know, Mom," April said. She glanced back at Jake, who still watched them with intense curiosity.

"I can't believe you're dating him," she said. "He's the catch of the whole campus. I used to see him on the beach, selling those little thingies he makes. What could he possibly see in you?"

"Thanks, sweetheart," Maggie said, heart sinking. "I appreciate your confidence in your old mom. Never let it be said that my daughter puts me on a pedestal."

SEVERAL YARDS AWAY, Jake watched as Maggie and April whispered viciously to each other, as if they were more than casual acquaintances from an aerobics class. Something wasn't right. He seriously doubted that the girl, who looked to be about fourteen months pregnant, would have jumped around in aerobics this past summer. But why would they have lied?

Maggie glanced his way, lifted her hand in a light wave, and the laughter in her eyes told him there was nothing to worry about. If she had lied, there was a good reason, and it didn't really effect him one way or another. All that really mattered to him now was figuring out a way to gracefully leave this party so that he could . . . at long last . . . be alone with his date.

When she came toward him, smiling as she scuffed through the sand, he felt his heart flipping. This was silly, he thought. He was too old to get this infatuated with a woman on their first date, but then, Maggie was no ordinary woman. She was different.

"Would you mind if we left now?" she whispered, looking up at him with eyes that still made him smile. "The medicine I took is starting to make me drowsy."

"Of course," he said, glancing back at April. "Is everything all right?"

"Oh, with April? Sure. She was just telling me about her husband losing his job. Come on, let's go."

Jake took Maggie's hand and pulled her back through the crowd, offering goodbyes to the key frat brothers who were throwing the party. Then, without putting on his helmet, he got on the Harley.

"Let's ride on the sand for a while without our helmets," he said. "I'll drive slow. I just like to feel the wind blowing through my hair when it's cool like this."

Maggie laughed, and the sound lilted across the water. "Sounds great."

She got on and they pulled away, but just before they got out of sight, Maggie looked over her shoulder. April was gaping at her mother riding off on a motor-cycle with a college beach bum, and again, Maggie's laughter competed with the sound of the engine. She only hoped that the shock wouldn't send April into early labor.

NOT FAR UP THE BEACH from where the party was held, Jake steered the Harley off the sand and around a small beach house. He pulled into a driveway, killed the engine and slid off the bike.

"Where are we?" Maggie asked, trying to finger comb her windblown hair.

"Home."

He saw the apprehension cross over her face, and for the first time it occurred to him that maybe it was too soon to take her home. Maybe it would frighten her away, and that was the last thing he wanted to do. The fact that she felt any apprehension at all endeared her to him, however, for he couldn't remember the last time anyone had balked about being alone with him. Maggie Conrad was a refreshing change. Her timidity only made him want her more, but at the same time, it forced him to move more slowly. Maggie was like a hummingbird—adventurous and flighty, but very, very cautious.

"I wanted to show you some of what I'm working on," he said, "but if you'd rather not . . ."

"No, that's fine," she said, slipping off the bike. "I'd like to see your work."

He took her hand and pulled her up the steps from the driveway to the house, unlocked the door and flicked on the light.

Maggie stepped inside and looked around at the walls covered with delightful pieces of art and photography and special treasures he'd no doubt found on the beach. Jake walked across the living room to the CD player, pressed a button and the lyrical sounds of the musician Yanni drifted across the room. Maggie had loved Yanni's music since she'd discovered him a year ago. It was romantic and timeless, sweet and sexy. Tonight it was the sexy part that made her a bit uncomfortable.

Jake came back for her and took her hand again. She savored the feel of his hand swallowing hers. It was rough and virile and tender all at once. He pulled her into a studio where several sand sculptures were in progress, all at the same stage like an assembly line, but on another table was something else—a piece of clay, still raw and unformed, except for one side, which was beginning to take shape.

"This is going to be a special piece," Jake said, abandoning her hand to touch the clay. "I'm waiting until the muse shows me exactly what's under all this. The touch and shape and texture…" His voice dropped with a sensual dreaminess that made her blood run warmer. "Then it'll just be a question of pulling off the layers covering it up… until the vision matches the reality."

"It sounds wonderful," Maggie whispered, as if she were standing in the presence of something reverent.

"It will be," he said. "You wait and see."

She met his eyes, and this time, hers were serious, pensive, as she gazed up at him. He was an enigma. A beach bum with a dream. A hack with a heart. A romantic with a vision.

And she liked him more than she'd liked anyone in a very long time.

As if he saw that realization taking hold in her mind, Jake narrowed the space between them and took both of her hands in his. He set them on his waist then touched her shoulders, all the while locking her eyes in his mesmerizing gaze.

"I've really had a good time being with you tonight, Maggie," he whispered.

"Me, too," she returned, unable to say more for fear that her voice wouldn't hold up.

He wet his lips, and Maggie felt her heart bursting with anticipation. Slowly—too slowly, so slowly, in fact, that she wanted to grab his head and jerk him down to her—he moved his face to hers.

When their lips touched, she felt as if the last barrel had clicked in a combination lock, the lock that had held all her emotions and feminine needs and sensual desires stored away. The lock that had helped her be the perfect example as a mother, but had denied her her own hopes and dreams.

She wondered if he felt the emotions flooding through her, the almost crazed desire, the desperate craving for more as the kiss moved deeper. Then all at once, her fears disappeared and she realized that he, too, was experiencing something similar, for as his hands closed around her and he crushed her against him, she felt his heart hammering against her chest, a slight tremor in his hands, and she heard a barely audible moan escaping from his throat.

At that moment Maggie wanted him more than she'd ever wanted that college degree or the independence she'd grown to love or the solitude she'd grown so comfortable with over the past months. For that instant she wanted him more than she had ever wanted anything and yet a voice inside her cried out that it wasn't like her to fall into bed with a virtual stranger. It wasn't right. It wasn't something she could feel good about tomorrow.

And feeling good about herself was very important to her, because she had learned long ago that if she couldn't do it, nobody else would.

Slowly she withdrew from the kiss, embarrassed at her breathlessness. He didn't let her go, and she could feel the heat of his desire.

"I—I should really get home soon," she said. "School starts tomorrow, and..."

Disappointment ebbed in his eyes. "I was hoping we could be together a little longer."

"Like...the whole night?" she asked softly.

His grin broke the tension. "Maybe."

She matched his grin and slipped out of his arms. "I couldn't do that, Jake. I barely know you."

"What better way to get to know someone?"

She gave him a look that said she was beyond that kind of logic. "I can think of a hundred better ways. Taking off my clothes wouldn't be required in any of them."

"You wouldn't have to take off your clothes. I could do it for you."

She felt her face burning with the heat of her own temptation, but she told herself she was too old to be taken in with sexy words. She knew better.

"I have to go home," she said. "Really."

Jake slumped back against the wall and grinned longingly at her. "You're tough, aren't you?"

Maggie smiled. "Not nearly as tough as you might think."

"Then you did want it, too?"

She thought for a moment, trying to decide whether admitting to her desire would cause more problems than it would solve. Finally she decided to hedge. "I'm a normal, functioning woman, Jake. And I'm probably no more immune to that special Jake Abel charm than any other woman is. I'm just smarter."

He obviously liked her answer, for his grin grew more amused. "I didn't know there was a special Jake Abel charm."

"Yes, you did," she said. "And you know how to use it, too. But that's okay. I'm no teenage virgin. I can handle it."

"You can, can't you?" he asked, still amused. "You know, I hate to admit this, but I'm not going to sleep until I get you into bed."

"Then you're going to find yourself pretty exhausted," she said with a coy smile.

"Are you saying you'll never sleep with me?"

She laughed at his boldness. "I'm saying that I will never sleep with a stranger. And it takes me a long time to get to know someone well enough to reveal myself to him that way."

"Then what are we talking?" he teased. "Two, three weeks?"

She tried to shoot him a deprecating look, but he took her hand and laughed aloud.

"If you're not careful, Maggie Conrad, I just might make you one of my goals in life."

"That's scary," she said as she opened the door and started out down the steps. "I hate to see you set yourself up for disappointment."

"It's a matter of perspective," he said. "I consider it a challenge." He helped her get onto the Harley, then set the helmet on her head and buckled it. Bending down, he kissed her again, then winking, he pulled his own helmet on. "And Maggie, darlin', it's a goal I promise to reach. Everybody has to have a dream, you know."

Chapter Four

Her dreams regarding Jake wavered precariously between anxiety and despair for the next few days, and finally, Maggie had to admit that those feelings had one major source.

Cellulite. The curse of women over the age of twenty-five, and many under that age, as well. The thought of it loomed over Maggie for the next few days, usurping any thoughts of her new classes or her schoolwork or the people she was meeting on campus. Cellulite! Those ugly, cottage-cheesy dimples that made her cringe in fear at the very thought of her taking her clothes off for Jake.

She couldn't go out with him again. That was all there was to it. She couldn't risk his getting closer, melting her heart into her toes, making her lose her head. The thought of his reaction to her aging body was more than she could bear.

"Put your clothes back on, darlin', and we'll pretend this never happened."

He would say the words with all the charm he could muster, considering his disgust, and she would maintain her dignity and remind herself that not one of those teeny-boppy bikini-clad skin-and-bones girls he dated had her knowledge and class. The knowledge and class of a grandmother.

No way, Maggie thought, cutting across the campus between the Fine Arts and Math buildings along the path Jake had outlined for her on that first day. She wouldn't even risk it. The less she saw of him, the better. In fact, if she never went out with him again, she'd never have to worry about it. She would simply save herself for some nearsighted professor who was older and looked worse than she did. The problem with that, however, was that she hadn't been attracted to a single one of her professors yet. All she had been able to think of was keeping the time open in case she ran into Jake.

Now she couldn't believe how idiotic she had been.

She heard someone running behind her and eased to the edge of the sidewalk to let him pass. But the steps slowed behind her, and in her ear she heard Jake's deep, virile rumble.

"How's the sexiest woman on campus doing today?"

She looked up and instantly grinned at the laughter in his eyes, and she wondered if he'd had them checked lately. Maybe he was as nearsighted as she needed him to be. "Well, I don't know. Why don't you point her out to me and I'll ask her?"

He set his arm possessively across her shoulder and fell into step with her. "You know who I'm talking about. The goal I've set myself. The one I've been having some pretty interesting dreams about lately."

"Hey, you said you wouldn't sleep. And now you tell me that you're having dreams?"

"It's restless sleep," he amended. "And the dreams are pretty darn close to what the real thing would be like."

"Are they?" she asked skeptically, without adding that she wondered if his dreams sculpted her body perfectly or if she still had the imperfections that had turned her own dreams into nightmares. "Well, enjoy them, since they may be as close as you ever come to finding out."

He laughed, as if delighted with her put-down. "You're something, Maggie. So when can I see you again? Friday night?"

She thought for a moment and realized the same panic that had made her try to cancel her first date with him. April and Steve would likely be home Friday night, and she wasn't ready to spring them on him. One disaster at a time, she thought. "I don't think so. I have something else I need to do that night."

He threw his hand over his heart, as if she had carelessly speared it. "Turned me down. I can't believe it. I'm starting to think you don't like me, Maggie Conrad."

She smiled. "It isn't that. Really."

"Then pick another time. Any other time."

She searched her brain for April's schedule and remembered that April and Steve went to Lamaze classes on Saturday mornings. They'd be gone at least two hours. Enough time for Jake to pick her up. As for bringing her home, she would just not invite him in if they were there.

"All right," she said. "How about Saturday morning?"

"Great. We can spend all day together getting to know each other, and by Saturday night, you'll be all over me. I'll have to fight you off, because you could never respect me if you got me into bed that soon. But since I'm such a weak individual, there's no telling how hard I'll fight. I might wind up giving in—"

"Wait a minute!" she said, cutting him off. "I said Saturday morning. I didn't say anything about bed or night or anyone fighting anyone off."

"Damn, you're tough," he said. "All right. I'll pick you up at ten, and we'll play it by ear. Sound okay?"

She laughed and looked away, struggling to see the wisdom in this. What if she got more attached to him and all of his prophecy came true? What if she fell for him and came away with a broken heart, like that of a fourteen-year-old girl bitten by puppy love? And why did she suddenly feel so young and out of control?

Maggie sighed, a sigh that Jake interpreted as reluctance, but that really meant surrender to her own temptations. "All right. I guess that'll be all right."

"You're sure?" he asked. "I don't want to force myself on you if you really don't like me."

She knew he was fishing and she grinned up at him. "I do like you, and I don't feel forced."

"You like me, huh? So you admit there's a maddening attraction here that's bigger than both of us? One that might free either of us from the responsibility of controlling ourselves?"

His insufferable persistence made her laugh, and she shook her head. "No, I don't admit that, Jake. Can you handle a day of companionship without the hope of sex? Is that something someone like you can comprehend?"

He considered it for a moment, as if he wasn't sure, but finally he said, "Yes, I think I can handle that. I'm

not saying I like it particularly, but, darlin', I'd rather
have you with your clothes on than not at all.''

"Gee, that makes me feel so much better," she said
facetiously, but the words were really sincere. She did
feel better that she could be adamant about what would
not happen between them and he'd still want to be with
her. She tried not to ruin the moment by wondering
why.

He bent down and dropped a kiss on her cheek, then
winked and started away. "See you Saturday, then."

She only smiled as she watched him disappear into
the Fine Arts Building.

"ALL RIGHT, MOM," April said to Maggie Saturday
morning as she stepped out of the bathroom. "You can
go out with him one more time, but be careful where
you go. Just don't let any of my friends see you with
him."

Maggie shot her daughter an irate look. "Honey, I
don't think I need your permission to go out with anyone."

"But, Mom, it's so embarrassing! Think of how it
looks!"

Maggie tightened the towel around her and gaped at
her daughter. "April, I've worried how it looks for the
past eighteen years. That's why I've rarely dated anyone. That's why I've been alone all this time. I was always afraid of looking like the desperate divorcée. But
you know what? I'm tired of caring what people think.
It's time I learned how to have fun. And I can't think
of one reason that I don't deserve that."

"But, Mom, look how much older you are than him!
Can't you date some middle-aged man? I could just die
every time I think of you with him!"

"I'm not exactly ancient, April. I still have a few good years left in me, and Jake certainly doesn't think I'm all washed-up. What's so terrible about that?"

"What's so terrible? I'll tell you. My child's grandmother is going to be a woman who takes Psych 101, rides motorcycles to frat parties and dates a beach bum."

Her eyes sparkling with laughter, Maggie looked off into space, trying to picture it. "I like that," she said. "That's just the kind of grandmother I want to be."

"Well, that's not the kind of grandmother *I* want you to be!" April said. "I want my child to have a grandmother who bakes cookies and sews and rocks it to sleep at night. Someone nice and settled! *I'm* the one who's supposed to be discovering myself!"

Maggie took the towel off her head and shook it out. "April, I'm not trying to discover myself. I've already done that, and what I discovered was a woman who has done nothing for herself in the last couple of decades. It's not like I'm going to marry the guy! I just want to go out with him and have a little fun! And I'm sorry if you can't accept that." She stroked the brush through her hair, then turned back to her daughter and pointed the brush at her. "I hope you'll live your life differently, April. I hope you'll go after your dreams while you're young and be everything you have the potential to be. I hope it doesn't take you twenty years to discover that you deserve more, but if it does, it won't be too late. It won't be too late until they shovel dirt into your grave—and I'm not dead yet!"

April glared back at her, and when Steve called, "April, time to go!" she backed out of the bedroom.

"Mom, just be careful, okay? It's not like it was when you were my age. Dating's a lot different now. Don't be afraid to say no, okay?"

Somehow, the seriousness in April's face, not to mention the reinforcement of her words evident in her stomach, struck Maggie as funny, and struggling not to smile, she said, "Thanks, honey. I'll remember that."

April waddled out, rubbing her tummy, and Maggie plopped down onto her bed. Finally, she let the laughter play out of her, and when it was gone, she lay staring at the ceiling, thinking of Jake.

Don't be afraid to say no.

The thought occurred to her that what she feared the most was not *wanting* to say no. What if she wanted to say yes? What if she couldn't fight it?

The towel fell off of her, and she looked down at her bare body, trying to see it through Jake's eyes. And suddenly all her fantasies popped like a soap bubble.

No, the best thing she could do was keep him at bay. She would enjoy his company, with no hope of it leading to anything else. She would pal around with him, neck a little and stop when it started heading where it couldn't.

And then she would come home and take cold showers and beat her head against her pillow until the desire diminished from her mind.

JAKE LAID THE LAST LOG in his fireplace, stood back and tried to imagine the fire that would rage to life when he brought Maggie back here tonight. It would create the perfect ambience for what he had planned— even if he did have to turn the air conditioner on to keep them from sweltering before the fire. Ambience

was the main thing. Women couldn't resist it, any more
than he could resist the strong pull of fate he'd felt
since the first moment he'd seen her tumbling into his
life.

He went to the art pad he'd left open on his kitchen
counter and smiled down at the sketch he'd done of her
last night. "It's already mapped into our future, darlin'," he told the picture. "Your surrender is just a
matter of time. Then I'll be the captive, but that's just
fine with me."

Humming "Tonight's the Night" under his breath,
he took the pad back into his studio, tossed it onto his
worktable. Then going back into the kitchen, he withdrew the single pink rose he'd kept there all night and
laid it across her place mat on the table. Digging into
his jeans pocket, he pulled out a book of matches and
laid it beside the candelabra. Stepping back, he ad-
mired the look of the table. It was perfect, he thought.
By the time Maggie went home tonight, he'd have her
eating out of his hand. *If* she went home at all.

He checked the bedroom and straightened the com-
forter over the clean sheets he'd gotten up early to wash
this morning. He wondered if she liked cuddling in her
sleep, or if she was one of those who kicked off the
covers and hugged the edge of the bed. He hoped she
liked to cuddle, because he knew he wouldn't be able
to keep his hands off her for that long. He had fanta-
sized too much about holding her all night, feeling her
warmth and listening to her breathing, smelling her
hair and tangling her legs in his. He wondered if she'd
feel self-conscious sleeping nude, or if he'd have to loan
her a T-shirt. He could live with either choice, he
thought with a smile. The truth was that he didn't mind
if she slept in a turtleneck and long johns. Just shar-

ing the intimacy of sleep in his arms was the main thing. Sex would be a bonus.

He began to whistle the tune that Rod Stewart had made famous, then chuckled as he realized his other Stewart favorite was "Maggie May"—about an older woman and younger man. Fleetingly he wondered if Rod's Maggie had been anything like *this* Maggie. Song inspiring, dream inspiring, awe inspiring.

He turned on one lamp in the corner of the bedroom, set the station on the radio for the soft, easy music he could turn on quickly, then walked through the house once more to check for anything he could have forgotten. He turned the lights down low, grabbed his helmet and started out to confront the morning.

"Eat your heart out, Rod," he said as he straddled his bike and headed out of the driveway. "This Maggie's mine."

"WHERE ARE WE GOING?" Maggie yelled over the roar of the Harley and the wind.

"It's a surprise," Jake called back to her. "Just hold tight."

As if the command had been a physical one, she tightened her hold on his waist and peered over his shoulder, squinting in the sunlight and trying to guess where they were heading. The only thing she could remember on this side of town was the airport, and she couldn't imagine why he'd be taking her there.

But as the tower loomed into sight and he turned into the small airport, she realized that was exactly where they were going.

Jake pulled the bike into a parking space in front of the terminal and pulled off his helmet. His grin was wry and secretive, and Maggie frowned suspiciously at him.

"Don't tell me, let me guess. You're taking me to Paris for the weekend."

His grin was even broader. "Darlin', if I had the money, I'd do it."

He took her hand and helped her off the motorcycle. Self-consciously, she finger combed her hair. "What then? Why are we at the airport?"

"Well, I can't afford Paris, but how about Miami?"

"What?"

"Lunch. There's this great little place I love in Miami. By plane, we can be there by noon."

Maggie stopped midstride and shot him another dubious look. "Is this a joke? Am I on *Totally Hidden Video?*"

He laughed and took her hand, pulling her alongside of him. "Come on, Maggie. Our magic carpet awaits."

"Oh, great. First a Harley, and now a magic carpet."

Jake pulled her through the terminal, then out the door to the tarmac where dozens of small planes were parked. "Carpet, no. Cessna, yes. That one over there. It belongs to a friend of mine, and he lets me use it occasionally."

"Use it?" she asked. "As in *fly* it? Are you a pilot? Licensed and everything?"

He chuckled as they reached the plane, and as he spoke, he began doing a preflight inspection of the plane. "Now, do you think I'd take you up in a plane I didn't know how to fly?"

"But you never mentioned it before. How long have you had your license?"

"About five years," he said, preoccupied as he checked under the plane. "I'm great at taking off. It's landing that I have a little trouble with."

Maggie started to back away. "Uh-uh. I'm not going anywhere with you in that."

Laughing, he reached out for her hand. "Come on, Maggie. I was kidding. I'm a terrific pilot."

Skeptically, she watched as he climbed up onto a wing, opened the door and reached down for her. "Come on, get in. A woman who can drive a Harley like you can shouldn't be afraid of a little old plane."

Maggie took his hand obediently and stepped up onto the wing. "Are you really taking me to Miami for lunch?"

"Where else would we eat?" he asked, grinning.

As if that answer cleared up everything, Maggie stepped into the plane and took the passenger's seat. The instrument panel was more than a little intimidating, and the controls frightened her. Again, she looked at Jake and said a silent prayer that he really did know what he was doing.

He winked at her then and laughed out loud. "Relax, Maggie. If you calm down, I might even let you fly once we get in the air."

"I—I don't think so."

"Well, at least you could try landing it. Your depth perception might be better than mine. Miles, feet, I keep getting them mixed up." He waited for a reaction, and when he saw her face go pale, he laughed aloud again. "It's a joke, Maggie. A joke."

Maggie tried to find something about it amusing as her fingernails bit into the seat and the plane began to move down the runway.

As soon as Maggie saw Jake's ease in flying the plane, her fears subsided and she relaxed and allowed herself to watch him with amusement. "How in the world did you learn how to fly?"

Jake laughed. "My best friend is a flight instructor. He's the one who owns this plane. Before he got married, we used to take off every weekend in it. Now he's immersed in fatherhood, and he doesn't have much time for it. He's glad to see me use it now and then, as long as I pay for the gas."

"That's great," she said, shaking her head. "You just never know about people."

"What do you mean?"

"I just mean...you don't look like a pilot. But then, I guess we don't know each other all that well, do we?"

"Well, we can change that easily enough," he said. "Let's see. What can I tell you? I'm a big brother to two sisters, and my parents are alive and well and still married after thirty years. I was an overachiever in high school, so you can imagine the disappointment I've been to my parents. It's kind of hard to brag to your friends about your son the beach bum."

"You're not a beach bum," Maggie said. "You're an artist. A good one."

"Yeah, but they're not quite as open-minded as you. They're easily impressed by money, though, so to prove I'm not entirely good-for-nothing, I try to buy them things like video cameras and microwaves for Christmas and birthdays." He shot her a grin. "You know, they'd really like you."

"Why? I don't have money."

"No, but you have that look they like. You know, that look of culture and sophistication. Plus, you wear more clothes than most of the women they've seen me with."

That dimple reasserted itself in his cheeks, and Maggie laughed. "Gee. I can't wait to be categorized with the Bimbo Brigade. Sort of gives me a whole new self-image."

"It should," he said. "But don't worry about being categorized. The Bimbo Brigade can't hold a candle to you. As a matter of fact, if my parents met you, they might decide that I'm still an overachiever in one area of my life. It might be enough to make them forgive my career choices."

"I wouldn't call dating me overachieving," she said. "In fact, I'm sure you have plenty of more interesting women waiting in the wings for you."

"Oh, thousands. But none more interesting, and certainly none more fun. And don't knock it. I have impeccable taste. Everybody says so."

"Everybody who?"

"Everybody who knows my high standards in women. So high, in fact, that I rarely call for second dates."

"Uh-oh."

"Don't worry, kiddo. You've already passed the second-date test or we wouldn't be here. I'm the one in hot pursuit of this relationship."

"And what happens when the pursuit becomes a conquest?" she asked. "Do you lose interest then?"

"Well, I can't say for sure, since that's purely hypothetical, but I'd guess that conquering you might be paramount to an addiction. One of those lethal kinds where you'd sell everything you had, borrow, beg and steal for one more fix. And incidentally, it would be a toss-up as to which of us would be the conqueror."

Maggie grinned out her window, shaking her head. "I know I've said this before, but you're good. They must have Casanova classes in that fraternity you used to belong to."

"We're talking real chemistry, darlin'. You can't take a class to learn simple honesty."

"And that was probably on the final exam. How to Make Your Lines Sound Sincere. You graduated at the top of your class, didn't you?"

Jake laughed. "You're something else, you know that, Maggie? You make things real hard for a poor guy whose every waking thought revolves around you."

It was Maggie's turn to laugh. "Please. No one's ever given me that much thought."

He reached across the seat and took her hand. "Hey, just because you were once married to a thoughtless, unfaithful, low-class bum doesn't mean you rate that."

She snapped her eyes back to him. "How did you know all that?"

"Things you've said about the types you were attracted to, and the idle comments about infidelity. Not to mention your inferiority complex when it comes to other women. Someone's done a pretty heavy job on you, darlin'."

She swallowed the emotion suddenly blocking her throat. "You've gleaned all that just from the few times we've been together?"

"I'm a good listener, Maggie. I never miss anything you say. And it doesn't take a genius to figure out that you're a maddeningly attractive woman who goes at life with a gusto and isn't above trying something new now and then, in spite of the things that have held you down."

Maggie blew out a breath of astonishment at the inaccurate description. "Now that's a perfect example of how wrong people can be about each other."

"Wrong? How can I be wrong? You're in a plane with a man you hardly know, aren't you? You drove my Harley. You went to a frat party, and if that isn't a risk, I don't know what is."

"I did, didn't I?"

She looked out the window, at the clouds frothing just above them and the Florida coastline below. "But those were isolated instances. Usually I'm very predictable and boring. Once you really know me, you'll see that."

"I can't wait to really know you, Maggie. And leave it to me to judge whether you're boring."

A moment of silence followed, and he reached over and took her hand. "So tell me something I don't know about you. Something that will surprise me."

She looked over at him, wondering which secret she'd kept from him should be the first to be confessed. The one about her pregnant daughter or the one about her age? Sighing, she let go of his hand. "Well, you probably don't know that I have a daughter."

"A daughter? Really? Why haven't I seen her?"

"She hasn't been home when you've come by," Maggie said evasively. "Her name's April." She looked at him, waiting for him to make the connection with the April he'd met at the party, but he didn't.

"April. That's pretty. Does she ever see her dad?"

"Are you kidding?" She looked out the window and thought of the man who had abandoned her and their child so many years ago, the moment he'd found someone he liked better. "We don't even know where he is. Probably in some commune in Canada growing pumpkins for a living."

"And you never remarried?"

She shrugged again, a gesture she knew she used when emotions welled up in her. "No, I was too busy with April. It never seemed like the right time to get into a relationship."

"And now?"

Jake's probing question brought her eyes back to him again. "And now...April requires more space than attention. She's embarrassed by her mom."

"Oh, I remember that age. When I was twelve or thirteen, I used to duck into the car every time we passed a friend. I didn't want them to see me with my mom. I preferred to have them think I didn't have one."

Maggie laughed, but beneath that amusement came a faint wondering. Did he think April was twelve or thirteen? She decided to leave it at that, for she wasn't ready to disclose everything just yet.

"There's the airport," he said, taking the radio mike off its hook. He looked over at her and gave her a wink. "You ready to land this baby?"

"You do it this time," she teased, "and I'll do it on the way home."

"Okay," he said, "but you asked for it. Oh, and by the way, I should tell you that I'm taking what you said a few minutes ago as encouragement."

"What did I say?"

"Something about *when* our relationship goes from a pursuit to a conquest. I didn't miss that, Maggie. You didn't say *if*, you said *when*."

She tried to suppress her grin, but her efforts were futile. "If I recall, Jake, you said that was purely hypothetical. You were right."

"Well, I'd say it's time to move from hypothetical to fact. I have big plans for today."

Something inside Maggie tensed and she sat up straighter in her seat. "Jake, I hope you don't think—"

Jake grinned. "I don't *think* anything, Maggie. I just feel. And I thought you should be warned that the day holds a lot of promise. We both have a lot to prove, darlin'. And today's the day we're gonna do just that."

Maggie gaped at him, unable to speak, as he chuckled lightly and began their descension into the Miami airport. But as they did, she knew that even cold reality would no longer be a sanctuary. Jake couldn't be held off much longer, and the truth was, she wasn't sure she wanted him to be.

Chapter Five

"Come on. That car over there is for us." Jake grabbed her hand and helped Maggie down from the plane to the tarmac. She looked in the direction in which he'd gestured and saw a small Honda Civic waiting with a teenage girl standing beside it, waving toward them.

"Is that a rental car?"

Jake laughed. "No. I had someone pick us up."

"Pick us up? Who knew we were coming?"

He only grinned as they approached the girl—a tiny blonde who looked about eighteen—and before he could answer, she ran up to him and threw her arms around his neck. "You're late," she said, though her tone was anything but accusatory. "I pictured you lying dead in the Gulf with sharks circling the wreckage."

"Chill out, sis," Jake said, returning the embrace and dropping a kiss on her cheek. "You're getting to be just like Mom."

Maggie caught her breath. "Sis? Jake, is this your—"

"My baby sister," he said. "Rachel, this is Maggie."

Unexpectedly, Rachel threw her arms around Maggie's neck, as though she'd known her for years. "It's so good to meet you. I've been hearing about you for months!"

"Months?" Maggie asked skeptically.

Jake chuckled. "Sis, I haven't *known* her for months."

"Weeks, then."

"Sorry," Maggie said. "Try days."

"All right," Rachel confessed, throwing up her hands. "The truth is that I haven't heard anything at all about you. All any of us knew is that Jake was bringing a lady with him. Which, in itself, is radically significant, and it's got the whole family running around like crazy."

"Then let's go and put them out of their misery." Jake opened the car door, and Rachel jumped into the back seat. When he closed the door, Maggie caught his arm.

Her face was sober when he looked at her. "Jake, you didn't tell me you were bringing me to meet your family. You said you were taking me to a restaurant you liked here."

"No, I said there was a great little place to eat here. My mother is the best cook in the state, bar none."

He reached out to open her door, but she stopped him again. "Jake, you deliberately misled me. I'm not ready to meet your family."

"Why not? It's just for lunch, and then I had some other places to take you. Don't worry. Meeting my family doesn't imply some kind of commitment. It's no big deal."

"But you haven't had the chance to warn them. Don't you think they'll be a little shocked?"

The confusion on his face was genuine. "About what?"

"About the age difference. This isn't the kind of thing you just spring on people. It's too obvious."

He leaned against the car and cocked his head. "Yes, it's obvious that you're a little older than me, but not that much, Maggie. You're just a little squirt of a thing, and you'll have fourteen-year-old eyes even if you live to be eighty."

"But, Jake, we hardly know each other and—"

Jake pushed off from the car and glanced into the back seat, where Rachel was trying to look away, as if she didn't know they were arguing. "Look, if this is a problem, we don't have to go to my parents' house. Truth is, I wanted to show you off a little, but if it makes you uncomfortable, we can skip it."

Maggie let out a heavy breath and turned away, running her fingers through her hair to combat the wind. Show her off? Was he crazy? What would his parents think?

Still, the fact that he would even say such a thing moved her in a way she didn't want to confront, and she found that she couldn't work up much anger toward him. Finally she sighed and turned back around. "All right, we'll go. But I'm warning you, they're going to hate me. Your mother will probably ask me my intentions, and your father will ask *you* what on earth you see in me—which, incidentally, is an answer I'd like to hear myself. And they'll both tell me to leave their son alone and go out with men my own age."

"I'll take that chance," he said, taking her hand. "Calm down, Maggie. My parents aren't hard on anyone but me. I told you they'll love you. Otherwise you wouldn't be the first woman I've ever brought home since I moved away."

As that last bit of information—which Maggie had to agree was radically significant—began to sink in, he opened the car door and helped her inside. "Sorry for the delay, sis," he said to Rachel, "but we had a few world problems we had to solve before we could get going. You know, nuclear disarmament, the ozone layer, that sort of thing."

"I hope you solved them all," she said. "That ozone stuff is really starting to get me down."

Jake laughed and went around the car to get in himself. As they pulled out of the parking space, Maggie told herself that it wasn't going to be so bad. If they were all like Rachel, she didn't have a thing to worry about.

HALF AN HOUR LATER, Maggie realized that Jake's family members weren't all like anyone...least of all each other. His father was a staid, pipe-smoking conservative type in a business suit, the type she was quite sure would look down on an older woman dating his son. The first words out of his mouth after their introductions were, "Nice tan, son. Any day now you'll get walloped with skin cancer and shrivel up like a prune." He looked at Maggie, his face a little less disapproving. "You, on the other hand, are still pale. Which tells me that you weren't found on the beach and you probably have a real job."

"Oh, Horace, leave the poor girl alone," Jake's mother, Doris, rebuked. "Don't mind him, Maggie. Actually, he's paying you a very high compliment."

"Oh?" Maggie asked with a grin.

"Of course, I am, dear," Horace said, stoking his pipe. "You look like the type who could get my son in line. Maybe give him a little ambition. A little drive."

Maggie shot Jake a look and saw that he was grinning. "Oh, I think Jake does just fine. I'm probably his biggest fan."

"Some fan," he teased. "Dad, the first time we met, she had just steamrolled right over my exhibit in the university museum. Broke it into pieces."

"A girl after my own heart," Horace said, setting his arm around Maggie and ushering her along. "I've been wanting to break some of those sand sculptures into pieces for years. How he pays his bills playing in the sand is beyond me."

Maggie looked helplessly back over her shoulder as they went inside, and Jake let out a laugh that told her he couldn't be bothered by his father's criticism. It was a game they played, and Jake knew all the rules.

They were barely through the door when a woman of about twenty-two barreled out of the kitchen and threw her arms around Jake. "I couldn't meet you at the airport," she said, talking faster than Maggie could understand, "because I'm making the best gumbo you've ever tasted. It's Mom's recipe, but I've added a few things because my roommate is studying to be a chef and she showed me all these new tricks in the kitchen and—" The woman stopped cold and turned to Maggie, suddenly switching gears. "Oh, my God, you must be—"

"Maggie," Jake provided, his dimples cutting into his cheeks.

"Yes, Maggie!" the woman said. "I'm Becky— short for Rebekah. We've all got biblical names, you know. Anyway, I've been hearing about you for months!''

Maggie started to laugh, and Rachel shook her head. "Don't exaggerate, Becky. She knows we've never heard of her before in our lives."

Jake set his arm around Becky's shoulders and smiled down at her. "I've known her about a week, guys, but she's led such a sheltered life that I had to whisk her away to somewhere. I figured this was as good a place as any."

"Lord, yes," Doris said. "He finally found a woman whose wardrobe actually covers her body. No wonder he wanted us to meet you."

The approval on Doris's face, not to mention her voice, put Maggie instantly at ease, and she said a silent prayer of thanks that Jake's mother hadn't been a child bride. At least she was several years older than Maggie. And the fact that Rachel was April's age or younger was something she'd just have to put out of her mind.

As the family sat down, bantering back and forth so fast and loud that Maggie didn't know how any of them understood anyone else, she looked around the room. On one wall were several bookcases filled with little sand sculptures, clay statues and art pieces that looked remarkably like those she had seen in Jake's studio.

And suddenly she realized why he could stand his father's criticism so easily. It was because he didn't believe a word of it. His family was proud of his work, otherwise they wouldn't be exhibiting it the way they did.

Amazed and moved, Maggie wandered over to a shelf on which sand sculptures of dolphins and palm trees and flamingos stood, inviting admiration. A sculpture of Elvis singing in his famous jumpsuit acted as the centerpiece, but tucked over at one end was a clay sculpture of half of a little girl's face, a hand tucked under the chin, its fingers curled as naturally as if Jake had frozen the person herself.

Maggie turned around and saw that he had come to stand behind her and was watching her intently, gauging her reaction.

"Jake, is all this yours?"

He grinned. "Yeah. They probably just put it all out when they know I'm coming. 'Course, I have dropped in unexpectedly just to see, and it was still there. Either they're clairvoyant or they take some degree of pride in my work."

"Dream on, son," Horace said, going into the kitchen.

Jake chuckled and watched his father disappear. "He has one of my earlier clay pieces on his desk at work and a big oil painting I did on the wall behind his desk."

"But don't let that fool you," Doris said with a grin as she made to follow her husband. "We both hate that you're a beach bum."

Jake grabbed his mother and caught her in a crushing embrace. "Admit it, Mom. You know I have the potential to be a Michelangelo."

"Well, Michelangelo couldn't have captured Rachel that well," she admitted on a laugh. "Still, you never would have seen him peddling his wares to beachcombers, either. And your father's right. You're too tanned. It's not good for you."

She gestured for her daughter to help her in the kitchen, and Maggie picked up the sculpture of the little girl. "Is this what she was talking about? Is this Rachel?"

"Yeah," Jake said, his voice dropping to a reverent level. "I did that a few years ago when she was younger. You like that better than Elvis?"

Maggie didn't smile as she gazed on the clay sculpture, her eyes taking in every line etched into the child's face. "Jake, it's beautiful. I can't believe the same person..." Her words trailed off as she realized he might not see the compliment.

He set his hands on her shoulders and looked over her head at the sculpture. "I know. It's a far cry from dolphins and palm trees. That's why I'm back in school, Maggie. This is the kind of thing I really want to do."

She turned around and looked up at him, her eyes alive and sparkling. "And you should. You have to."

"Why?" he asked, his smile fading.

"Because you're gifted. No one who has a gift like that should settle for anything less."

For a moment he gazed down at her, his eyes poignantly sober. Finally he took her hand, and whispered, "Come on. Let's eat so Dad can get back to work. He's a CPA and meets with out-of-town clients on Saturdays. Then we'll cut out of here and do some things alone. You can grin and bear it for an hour or two, can't you?"

Maggie laughed. "It's not me. They may be in there biting their tongues right now, trying to figure out a nice way to tell you how crazy you must be for dating someone like me."

"A nice way?" Jake asked. "Are you kidding? No one in my family is anything less than blunt. If they had a problem with you, you'd have heard it by now."

"Yeah, sure. I'm supposed to believe they'd just come right out and say it?"

"Well, they've done it before. They were visiting me at my house once, and a girl in a bikini came up from the beach and knocked on my door and my father told her she wasn't welcome inside until she put something 'a little more appropriate' on. During that same visit, Carol—a girl I dated off and on for a while—came over to help cook for them and my mother asked her who the plastic surgeon was that gave her her breast implants."

"No!"

"She sure did. Which is why I never would have brought you here if I didn't know they'd love you."

"So why didn't they ask anything about my age?"

"Because they don't care. My father's twelve years older than my mother."

"That's different. He's a man."

"And it's scandalous if a woman is older?"

"It can be."

"But not in our case, because you don't look much older than me, darlin'. How many times do I have to tell you that?"

"A lot more," she said, "because I don't believe it."

Shaking his head and chuckling under his breath, he took her hand and pulled her into the kitchen.

MAGGIE COULD BARELY GET A word in for the next hour as she sat at Jake's family table, listening to the banter.

"And then when we started planning this wedding—by the way, Maggie, did Jake tell you I was getting married?" Before Maggie could shake her head, Becky answered for her. "Of course, he didn't, and I'll tell you why. He doesn't believe we'll go through with it, that's why."

"She's been engaged fourteen times," Rachel cut in.

"I have not," Becky said. "Only three other times. Twice to the same person, but I never could convince myself that he was good husband material, so I finally gave him the ax."

"She's so romantic," Rachel editorialized. "She puts them all through the Becky stress test, and if they pass, they get to put a ring on her finger."

"Which she may wear for weeks or months before she gives it back," Doris added.

"Oh, she doesn't give it back, do you, Becky?" her father said. "How do you think she bought that car she drives?"

"Daddy!"

Jake laughed and took his sister's hand. "Oh, it's not so bad, sis. You're just discriminating, that's all. With the big brother you have as a role model, it's just hard for all those other guys to measure up."

"You got that right," Becky said deadpan. "I've looked on every beach in Miami and haven't yet found anyone like you. I finally had to resort to lawyers and engineers."

"No doctors, though," Rachel said. "Becky said doctors cheat on their wives."

"All of them?" Maggie asked with a grin.

"Ninety-nine percent," Becky said with a tone of certainty. "I'm telling you, the health profession is rampant with infidelity. And not just doctors, either. From the chief surgeons right down to the janitors in the hospitals. They're all sleazeballs."

"She's had experience, in case you haven't picked up on that fact yet," Horace threw in for Maggie's sake.

"Had a raging crush on a pediatrician, until she found him in a lip lock with a physical therapist."

"Quit nursing school the next day," Becky admitted. "Decided I was too morally upstanding to consort with types like that. Besides, after I poured sugar in his gas tank, I didn't think I'd better show my face around there again."

"A woman scorned," Jake said, shaking his head. "Sis, we're rooting for you this time. But just in case, I wouldn't order the flowers until the last minute."

Becky slapped him playfully and turned to Maggie. "Have you ever been married, Maggie?"

"Yes, a long time ago. Well, not *that* long ago. Before. Once." She realized she was rambling, and her self-consciousness about her age was flashing like a neon sign all over her reddening face.

Becky leaned forward on the table and studied Maggie carefully, her eyes as wide as if she were being let in on some deep family secret. "So tell us. What happened?"

"Becky!" Jake said. "Don't you think that's getting a little personal?"

"No, it's all right," Maggie said, suddenly amused at Becky's straightforwardness. "I don't mind talking about it. Heaven knows it's ancient history." Quickly, she gave herself a mental kick for the choice of words. "My ex took off with some topless dancer he met in a bar. Well, she may not have been a topless dancer. Truth is, I don't know what she did. But she looked just like a bimbo to me."

Rachel took Maggie's hand and gave her a sympathetic look. "Does it still hurt?"

"Are you kidding?" Maggie asked on a laugh. "I send her a Christmas card every year thanking her for saving me from years and years of misery."

"Really?" Becky asked.

Maggie laughed. "No, not really. I don't even know where he is. And as long as he stays there, I'll be just fine."

"So what do you think?" Becky asked. "Should I get married or what?"

"Well . . . I don't know. . . ."

"Tell her no," Horace said, cutting in. "If she has to ask someone she's known an hour, the answer should be no. Hock the ring, Becky, and buy yourself a cruise. 'Course, then you'd probably fall for some Latin gigolo on some Bahamian island, and we'd wind up with two beach bums in the family." He gave his son a wink, which was received with laughter again.

"I'd rather marry a sand shaper than a paper pusher," Becky said, referring to her father's line of work.

"So do you have any children?" Rachel asked Maggie suddenly.

Maggie felt her face growing hot again, and she looked from face to face, her heartbeat suddenly accelerating. "Uh . . ."

"She has a daughter," Jake said. "April."

"April. That's nice," Doris said. "How old is she?"

Maggie shot Jake a look and saw that he was looking at her as intently as his family, waiting for an answer. It was a point-blank question, one that couldn't be evaded or misunderstood. And Maggie realized she had only one choice.

She had to lie.

"She's ten," she said, quickly taking a bite of gumbo to deter any further questions.

"Oh, what a cute age," Doris said. "They're right there between childhood and adolescence, and you never know which they're going to be from one day to the next. Where is she now?"

Maggie swallowed her bite and racked her brain for an answer. "At home. With a baby-sitter."

"A baby-sitter?" Jake asked. "You should have told me. We could have brought her with us."

Maggie choked on her next bite and quickly tried to recover. "No, she wasn't home when you came. She was...spending the night with a friend. The baby-sitter was going to pick her up. Besides, she hates heights. Airplanes scare her to death. So do motorcycles."

"Oh." He picked at his gumbo for a moment, then shot her a curious look. "What does she like?"

Fearing that he'd want to tailor some event to her fictitious little girl, Maggie quickly blurted out, "Nothing. I mean, she's a real couch potato. She mostly just likes TV."

"Well, I should rent some movies we could all watch," he said. "Better yet, you could bring her to my house one day and let her play on the beach."

"No, she hates water. And sand." Maggie looked at the confused faces around her, and added, "Actually, she really hates a lot of things. I have her in counseling. We're working on it."

"I'm glad to hear that," Doris said in a voice dripping with worry. "She sounds like a troubled child."

"Oh, no," Maggie said, laughing a little too loudly. "I didn't mean to give you that impression. Actually she's a very happy child. It just takes a bit of work to make her happy."

Jake frowned and stared at her, and she wondered if he believed a word of it. Quickly trying to rally, she turned to Rachel. "So Rachel. Are you in college yet?"

The conversation effectively made the turn she was looking for, and Maggie breathed a sigh of relief that the attention was off of her and her lies. At least for now. At least until Jake had cause to meet the real April in all her pregnant, married, homeless glory.

Until then, Maggie would just try to enjoy what little time she had left with him.

LATER THAT AFTERNOON, as they walked along the beach where Rachel had dropped them off, picking up pieces of driftwood that Jake could use in his work, Maggie tried to battle the depression that was hanging over her.

"I saw you talking to your family after I got in the car," she finally had the courage to say. "Were they asking you what you were doing with an old broad?"

Jake laughed out loud. "Actually, no. My father shook my hand and told me he hoped I had sense enough to keep you. My mother told me to get you to bring April the next time you come. And Rachel wants to get her hair cut like yours."

A slow grin crept across Maggie's face. "Really? You really think they liked me?"

"Maggie, there was never any question. Oh, I forgot about Becky. She's rethinking her engagement since you hesitated when she asked if she should get married. She thinks you've got a point."

"About what?"

"Who knows? She's crazy. They all are. But that's why they're fun."

"They are fun," Maggie said. "I'm glad you took me to meet them."

A strong breeze whipped through her blouse, molding the cloth to the shape of her breasts. Her hair bustled wildly around her face, and Jake reached out to push it out of her eyes. The touch was like an electric jolt that her heart had craved all day, and when he pulled her into his arms, she didn't resist. "Maggie, you're really getting under my skin, you know that?"

Standing on her toes, she joined her hands behind his neck and grazed his lips with her own. "You're not making it real easy for me, either."

His gentle smile was more devilish than his voice betrayed. "Making what easy?"

"Fighting you. This relationship. Keeping my head."

"I don't want you to fight me, Maggie. And I'd love to see you lose your head over me."

"But that would be frivolous and stupid," she whispered. "I don't want to fall for the wrong person."

"And who says I'm the wrong person?"

"That voice inside me that keeps reminding me how hopeless this is."

"Someone needs to shut that voice up," he whispered. "I think I might just have to work on that."

His kiss swept her from conscious reasoning to raw feeling, and she lost herself in his embrace. But there were no regrets as she felt herself slipping away, for she was safely anchored in the circle of Jake's arms. When he broke the kiss, Jake lifted her off her feet and drew in a deep sigh as he crushed her against him. "You're so little," he said, setting her back down. "So tiny. I love that."

"I'm not that little," she said. "You're just so big."
Bravely, she ran her hand down his chest, then up his
biceps. "I love the way you're built."

His grin was more evident in his eyes than on his lips.
"Are you saying that you like my body?"

"I guess that is what I'm saying."

"Well, that's good," he whispered. "Because there's
more of it. And I happen to be pretty crazy about
yours, too."

Her heart ran at breakneck speed, and she knew he
could feel it beating against him as her breasts crushed
into his chest.

"You know, I'm a breast man. And I really like
yours."

Her eyelids dropped to half-mast as she gazed up at
him. "You've never seen mine."

"I've seen their shape under your clothes," he said,
his breath growing heavier. "And I've felt them against
me when I've held you. I'd love to tear off your blouse
and fill my hands with them...."

Maggie took in a shaky breath. "Jake..."

He kissed her again, and this time she felt it right to
the tips of each breast and deep into her core, making
her want him more than she'd ever remembered wanting anything. She wondered just how far they could go
and still turn back. She wondered if ripping off her
shirt and feeling his hands on her breasts would push
them past the point of control.

Thankfully, it was broad daylight and there were
people milling around on the beach. She knew there
was no chance of any of that happening here.

He broke the kiss and let her go and taking her hand,
bent down to pick up the driftwood they'd gathered.
"You do crazy things to me, Maggie. You make me

want to do crazy things to you. But when I do them, I want us to be alone."

Maggie swallowed the hungry terror in her throat as he pulled her toward the hotel where they would catch the cab that would take them back to the airport.

IT WAS LATE AFTERNOON before they took off again and dusk when they landed. As the plane descended from the twilit sky, Maggie felt her heart falling, as well. She wasn't ready for the day to end. It had been too perfect. And as much fear as he'd planted in her heart of their being alone together, the disappointment at it not happening was even greater.

But before they reached the tarmac where he was to park the plane, Jake took her hand. "I hope you don't have to rush back, Maggie. I've planned a nice dinner for us."

"Dinner?" she asked. "But lunch was so nice. You don't have to—"

"I want to," he said. "I got up early and got everything ready. All I have to do is slap the steaks on the grill and we're in business. Can your daughter do without you a little longer?"

"April's in good hands," Maggie said, feeling a slight tug of guilt at the lie she had so easily concocted. "I'd love to have dinner with you."

But as she followed him out of the plane and saw the serious look on his face—that look that said he would like nothing more than to kiss her right here in front of everyone who cared to look, that look that promised to free her breasts from the clothes that confined them, that look that said he would get her into his bed the moment they got behind the doors of his house—she felt a slight stirring of panic. But it left as quickly as it came, for as she considered her alternative—going home and saying good-night—she decided that she would take the risk. She wasn't ready to leave Jake just yet.

There was no mistaking the ambience he had especially created for her, and she had no delusions that he'd done it all for a platonic evening. Jake Abel had other things on his mind.

But if moral fortitude wasn't enough reason—and Maggie doubted it could compete with Jake Abel's arms and his deep, probing kisses—then she only had to recall the inhibitions she had about her body. That was enough to keep her clothes on. The thought was like a splash of ice water directly in her eyes.

When she found the rose on her plate and he took the bloom and put it in her hair, tears came to her eyes.

They talked quietly over dinner, with the sound of Yanni playing his romantic instrumentals as candlelight flickered and shadows bounced against the wall.

When they had finished, Maggie began to clear the table. Jake grabbed her hand. "No way," he said. "I worked too hard setting this mood to have you destroy it with clashing plates and running water."

"Mood?" she asked facetiously, setting the plates back onto the table. "What mood?"

He slid his arms around her and with his lips only centimeters from hers, whispered, "This one. The one I'm in. The one I hope you're in."

His kiss startled her with its urgency, but the frustration at having been so intimate with him today without really having the chance to follow through on it had welled too deeply inside her. She wanted him as much as he wanted her, she thought. She wanted to touch him, to taste him, to breathe him....

His hands moved low over her hips, pulling her closer against him, and she felt his tumescence through his clothes, warning her that this was not a game. With a feeble effort, she tried to pull away, but he only pulled her closer.

His kiss deepened and Maggie felt something snap loose in her heart, that thing that restrained her and made her think. And once all thought was banished, she was left again with only feelings. Deep, urgent, hungry feelings.

She stood on her toes and slid her arms around his neck, then suddenly felt him lowering her to the couch. Her back fell against it, and he was beside her, fumbling with the buttons of her blouse, slipping his leg between hers, sliding one big hand over her hip.

He opened her blouse and slipped his hands inside. It slid over one budding nipple, and she shivered from her core. He broke the mesmerizing kiss and dipped his face to her breast, licked and suckled, stirring something alive in her that she had forgotten existed.

"I knew they would feel this way," he whispered, his breath sending goose bumps whispering over her skin. "I knew they would taste just like this."

His tongue flicked over her, and she shivered and told herself that now was the time to pull back, before things went any further. But she waited, savoring just one more minute of the luxury of his ministrations, then another and another, until she had forgotten her resolution and grew lost in his caresses.

Then suddenly he was unzipping her slacks, and it occurred to her that he couldn't get her out of them fast enough, that she wanted nothing more than to feel his bare skin against hers, their bodies sliding together, uniting....

The first of her doubts slipped back into her consciousness, doubt that she could please him the way he expected, doubt that he would be satisfied, doubt that she could even compare to all the other women he'd known. If she slept with him and he never called her again, could she honestly deal with the rejection?

Age. It all boiled down to her age, she thought miserably. It was the one factor that would do her in. The one thing that would be glaringly obvious when he saw her undressed. The one thing that would make her look like an idiot for ever consorting with him in the first place.

She grabbed his hand and stopped his progress, and he looked up at her, his eyes smoky hazed and longing.

"Maggie, I want you," he whispered. "You're driving me crazy."

"No," she whispered. "It's too soon."

"But we've been together all day," he said, as if that satisfied her argument.

Smiling sadly, she sat up to button her shirt. "I meant it's too early in this relationship. If we even *have* a relationship. I can't... I don't know you that well...."

"It's the best way I know to get to know each other," Jake said for the second time since they'd met. He watched her button the blouse, as shattered as a little boy watching his favorite hot-rod cars being thrown one by one into the ocean. "Maggie, I want to know you in every way. I want to be intimate with you."

"Intimacy has nothing to do with sex," Maggie said, struggling to recall all the arguments she had given April when she'd started dating. Unfortunately they hadn't done her much good, either. But then, April hadn't had the deterrent of a forty-year-old body.

"But intimacy leads to sex," he said. "Maggie, I think about you all the time. Every waking moment. I can't stand the days when I don't see you. I *dream* about you."

"Good," she whispered, touching his face. "I like that."

"But I want to do more than dream," he said.

"So do I," she admitted. Her mouth was dry, and she couldn't catch her breath. And her heartbeat still hadn't returned to normal. "But I can't. *We* can't. Not now."

He sat back, allowing her to straighten her clothes. The miserable look on his face would have been comical if she hadn't known that hers was equally miserable.

"I'm sorry, Jake."

"Don't be," he said, kneeling beside her on the couch and taking her hand in his. He pressed a kiss on her knuckle, then brought the palm to his cheek. "This only makes me want you more. You know that, don't you?"

"Then maybe some good came out of it."

They gazed at each other for a long, poignant moment, and finally, Jake got to his feet and helped her up. "It's been a terrific day," he whispered.

"I was supposed to say that," she said with a smile. "It was wonderful."

He touched her face with his artist's hand, tracing the shape and texture with feather-soft finger strokes. When he kissed her this time, it was sweet, moving, emotional, but not as sex driven as it had been before. She realized with great trepidation that his touch played havoc with more than her hormones this time. Now her heart was at stake.

Her eyes welled up with tears when he broke the kiss and, smiling, said, "Come on. I'll take you home."

Maggie couldn't speak as she followed him out of his house.

Her car was home when Jake pulled into the driveway, and Maggie knew that April and Steve were inside, probably curled up on the sofa, and that there would be no keeping Jake from seeing them if he came in. The day had been too perfect, too magical, and she didn't want to pop the bubble of fantasy they had created just yet.

She got off the bike, handed him her helmet and pressed a kiss onto his lips. "I had a great time, Jake," she whispered, hoping he would accept her goodbye here instead of walking her to the door.

But Jake had other plans. "Do you have any aspirin? I'm getting a headache. Must be my hormones. You know, all revved up and no place to go."

Maggie feigned regret and shook her head. "No, I don't think so."

"Sure, you do," Jake said. "I bought you a jumbo bottle just last week when you were sick."

"Oh, yeah." She looked toward the house and wondered how she could get in there before Jake and force April and Steve to hide under the beds.

"If it's your daughter you're worried about," he said, as if he read her mind, "I'm really not a monster around kids. Some of them really like me. Especially ten-year-olds. They think I'm cool."

Feeling a surge of guilt at the lie she had let go so far, Maggie dropped her head and studied her shoes a little too carefully. Some moral voice inside her cried out that it was wrong to lie about one's own child. Pretending that April didn't exist was tantamount to *wishing* she didn't exist, and that was a grave sin for a mother to commit. She told herself that if a man couldn't accept her for what she was, she didn't need to be around him, anyway.

But then another voice—a more familiar one—chimed in its opinion that a little harmless lie was not the same as wishing her daughter out of existence. It was merely wishing away a decade of birthdays.

"All right," Maggie said, her mind searching frantically for a way to handle this. "Let's go get you some aspirin."

Jake got off the bike and ambled to the door behind her, and as she touched the doorknob, she prayed that April wouldn't call her Mom. Her only hope was if she was the first one to speak.

She opened the door and stepped inside to see April and Steve cuddling on the couch, just as she'd expected. Before they could say a word, Maggie blurted out, "Jake, I'd like you to meet my baby-sitters, April and Steve."

"Baby-sitters?" Steve asked with a laugh as he came to his feet to shake Jake's hand. April frowned up at her mother without saying a word.

"April?" Jake asked, looking down at the pregnant girl on the couch. "Didn't I meet you at the Gamma Phi party?"

Maggie laughed too loud. "Of course. I'd forgotten. That's where I asked her to start baby-sitting for me."

Jake looked perplexed and frowned over at Maggie. "I thought you said April was your daughter's name."

"Yeah," April echoed. "That is your daughter's name, isn't it?"

Maggie faked a theatrical laugh. "Coincidence.
That's why little April likes her so much." As she
spoke, Maggie patted April's shoulder affectionately.
Only she and April were aware of the warning grip
Maggie had on her daughter. April had the good grace
not to wince, and Maggie said a silent prayer that—if
nothing else—her daughter had learned the art of de-
ceit from her old mom. "Is little April asleep already?" Maggie asked.

Big April nodded and shot Steve a warning look that
said, *Yes, I realize she's snapped, but if we want a roof
over our heads, we'd better play along.*

"Yeah, right," Steve said. "She's sound asleep. You
wouldn't even know she was in the house." He snickered at his cleverness, and Maggie's face reddened.

"Darn," she said, smiling up at Jake. "I really
wanted her to meet you. Oh, well, maybe next time."

"Yeah," April said. "Next time we'll make a point
of keeping her up for you, Jake. Maggie's so proud of
her daughter."

Maggie caught the stinging barb and shot April another warning look. April and Steve only stared at her,
waiting for their next cue. "Well, thank you guys, for
watching her all day. I really appreciate it." Maggie
waited for them to get up and pretend to leave, but they
only stared. Clamping her teeth, she added, "You must
be anxious to get home."

"Oh, yeah." April shot to her feet and nudged Steve,
who still studied Maggie, no doubt devising ways of
turning this little stunt to his advantage. She could see
the amusement in his eyes. "Come on, honey."

"All right," Steve said. "Let's go...home." He
snickered again, and Maggie wanted to pick the brass

bird off the end table and hurl it at the back of his head.

Maggie sighed relief as they said their goodbyes to Jake, who didn't seem suspicious yet, but when Steve got to the door, he turned back with a grin. "Oh, wait. What could we have been thinking? You forgot to pay us!"

Maggie glared at him, and April covered her grin and struggled not to laugh. "Yes, well...I'll mail you a check tomorrow."

"No way," Jake piped in, reaching for his wallet. "Let me. I'm the one who kept Maggie out all day. How much does she owe you?"

"Twenty bucks," Steve said with a grin that dared Maggie to correct him.

Jake pulled out a twenty and handed it to him.

"Jake, don't give him that!" Maggie snatched the twenty out of Jake's hand, and both men looked at her, Jake with confusion, and Steve with a smugness that dared her to explain. She decided right then and there to devote the rest of her life to wiping that annoying smile off his face.

"Why not?" Jake asked. "They sat for her all day. It's the least I can do."

"Yeah, Mags," Steve said. "It's the least he can do."

Maggie bit her lip until she almost drew blood as Steve took Jake's money, and it occurred to her for the first time that her son-in-law could have a brilliant future in politics. Either that or the Mafia.

When they were gone, Maggie turned to Jake and smiled an overbright smile. "Now..." she said, out of breath.

As if he realized something was wrong but couldn't put his finger on what, Jake frowned and peered out the window, where Maggie knew April and Steve would linger until he was gone. She hoped they had the sense to hide behind some bushes in the backyard. But as soon as that image struck her, she was walloped with the absurdity of the whole charade. What kind of mother would make her child hide in the backyard for the sake of her love life? But then she told herself that it wasn't all that bad. It wasn't as though April really *was* a child anymore, and besides, she probably needed some fresh air. And she of all people would understand that desperate people do desperate things.

"How are they getting home?" Jake asked. "I didn't see a car."

"On foot," Maggie said quickly, disturbed at how easily these lies rolled from her lips. "They just live a block away."

Jake seemed satisfied with the explanation. "That's convenient."

"Yes, very," she said. "Now, let's see. We came in here for some aspirin."

She led him into the kitchen, hurriedly trying to find the bottle. She had no doubt that April and Steve were sitting in the backyard, watching their every move through the window. It made her nervous, and Jake saw it.

Taking her hands and turning her around to face him, he asked, "Darlin', what's wrong?"

She glanced self-consciously toward the window. "Nothing. I just can't find it...."

Jake reached into the open cabinet and withdrew the bottle. "Here it is."

"Oh, good." Hurrying, she filled a glass with water and thrust it at him, sloshing some onto the floor.

"Maggie, I think you're a little tired."

She nodded. "Yes, that's it. I'm exhausted."

He smiled and took the pills, then bent down and dropped a kiss onto her lips. "You're nervous about bringing a man home with your daughter in the house, aren't you?"

She closed her eyes and let out a deep breath. "You have no idea."

"Well, then I'll leave. I don't want to make you uncomfortable." He pulled her into a tight hug, and her emotions struggled between her need to bask in his embrace a little longer and her knowledge that her every move was being watched and remembered for future blackmail opportunities. "But I do want to meet her when you're ready."

She smiled and glanced toward the window through which she was sure April was peering. "Oh, I'm sure it's inevitable, if we keep seeing each other."

"*If* we keep seeing each other?" he asked. "Is there any reason why we wouldn't?"

"Only about two thousand," Maggie said with a heavy sigh. "For one thing, the night didn't quite end up the way you wanted."

"It ended up fine. Just played havoc with my libido, but like I said, it only makes me want you more. What else?"

"You might be tired of me after spending the whole day together."

"Tired of you?" He laughed aloud. "Maggie, Maggie, Maggie. The day I get tired of you is the day I take a long walk out the door of an airborne plane. It won't happen. Are you tired of me?"

"Oh, yeah," Maggie said. "I always get tired of men who fly me to Miami for lunch and whisk me around town on a Harley. The boredom is just too much."

Jake laughed, not at all convinced. "Well, if I'm not boring you and you're not boring me, maybe you'd better start preparing your daughter for meeting me. Because I plan on spending some time over here."

He pulled Maggie against him, kissed her again, then pushed her hair out of her eyes. "Have a good night, okay? Dream about me."

She felt that familiar emotion welling in her throat, and whispered, "I will."

Standing back, she watched as he cranked the Harley again and pulled into the street.

He was a block away before she started into the house. April and Steve were coming in the back door at the same time. "Great going, Mom," April said in her best wounded child voice, "sending us out to stand in the cold while you neck with your boyfriend."

"April, we were not necking!" Maggie tried to lower her voice and took a deep breath. "I really appreciate your going along with me on that, guys."

"You owe us one," Steve said.

"I beg your pardon?" Maggie asked, shooting him a murderous look. "You extorted twenty bucks from him, Steve. I'd say that's enough."

April bristled. "Twenty bucks for pretending we weren't related. Twenty bucks for hiding outside like thieves. Mom, what in the world was that all about?"

Maggie wished to God she didn't have to answer these questions now. Couldn't her daughter just accept that she'd had the need to hide her and leave it at that? "I just don't believe in disclosing everything right up front. I believe in keeping some secrets. You know. It gives you more surprises as you get to know each other."

"Give me a break. You don't want him to know how old you are." April's cynical words were a slap in the face, and Maggie knew she wouldn't slip past April as easily as she'd hoped.

"Why not, Grandma?" Steve asked on a laugh. "What's the problem?"

"He thinks my daughter's much younger," Maggie said with a hiss. "I'm just not ready to tell him differently. Look, I know it's silly. Downright ridiculous, really. But I can't help it."

April set her hands on her hips and looked down her nose at Maggie. "And just how long do you think you can keep up this charade?"

Maggie felt her face going crimson, and she mumbled, "I don't know."

"You don't know." April nodded like a matron pondering the folly of a child. "Well, let me tell you. Not much longer. One lie will lead to another, and pretty soon—"

"April, I don't need this!" Maggie cut in. "I don't want to talk about it anymore."

"All right, then," April said smugly, moving her hands from her hips to cross them over her stomach. "Then let's talk about something else. Like where you've been all day. And what you've been riding on."

Maggie gaped at her, not sure how to respond.

"Do you know how dangerous it is to ride a motorcycle?" April went on. "Besides that, you've been gone since morning. It's almost eleven!"

Thankfully, Maggie began to see the humor in the sudden role reversal and going back into the living room, she kicked off her shoes and plopped down in her favorite chair. April followed her, waiting for an answer.

"Mom, we didn't know what had happened to you. For all we knew, he could be an ax murderer."

Maggie laughed. "Trust me. He's not an ax murderer. Besides, you told me you knew him."

"By reputation," Steve said. "He's a real womanizer, Mags. I hope you didn't let him try anything on you."

Again Maggie let her laughter overtake her. "What is this? The Spanish Inquisition? It seems like I've heard this before. A year ago, as a matter of fact, only I was the mother and *April* was the daughter."

"Yeah, and look what happened to me!" April cried. "Mom, I'd die if you let that guy get you pregnant."

Now Maggie's laughter reached an uncontrollable level, and she clutched her stomach and let it overtake her. "I can't believe my pregnant daughter is giving me a lecture on birth control."

"Well, while we're on the subject, what *are* you using for birth control?"

"Cellulite!" Maggie blurted, still laughing.

April's eyebrows drew together. "What?"

Maggie rubbed her forehead and began to laugh again. "April, I refuse to discuss this with you. I'm forty years old and, despite what you think, I'm neither stupid nor crazy."

"Oh, no?" April asked. "Then I suppose rational, sane people always hide their children in the backyard when their dates come over?"

"You're not a child, April. It wasn't that big of a deal."

"But you did that because of the age difference, so you must realize how ludicrous it is for you to be dat-

ing him! What could you two possibly have in common?''

Maggie's amusement faded and she stared off into
space, reliving part of the day. ''He took me to Miami
for lunch,'' she said softly.

''Miami? How? That's six hours one way.''

''Not by plane, it isn't.''

April glared at her. ''He took you to Miami in a
plane?''

''Flew it himself,'' she said with a wry grin.

''Cool,'' Steve said. ''He's a pilot?''

''Yep. And we had a wonderful day.'' She smiled up
at her daughter, got up and grabbed her shoes. ''I'm
going to bed, April.'' Placing a kiss on her dismayed
daughter's cheek, she said, ''I'm sorry you don't ap-
prove, sweetheart, but that's life. I suggest you get used
to the embarrassment of it all, because Jake and I
might be spending more time together.''

''It's the backyard I'd better get used to,'' April
muttered. ''Do me a favor and let me know the next
time you want to hide me. I'll save us all the trouble
and find a cave somewhere.''

Maggie smiled at April's theatrics and turned to face
her daughter. ''April, I'll bring you out of the closet as
soon as I think he can handle it. Until then, what's
wrong with my enjoying a little romance?''

''So you think he'll dump you if he finds out about
me?''

Maggie sighed and her expression faded. She hadn't
wanted to express her fears that clearly, but April
couldn't have been closer to the truth.

''You do think that. That's just great. The relationship is doomed for failure, but when it fails, I'll get the
blame.''

"Nobody will blame anybody," Maggie said quietly. "If it's not meant to be, it's not meant to be."

As she walked out of the room, Maggie heard April lamenting to her husband, "I don't know what we're going to do with her."

And she remembered using those same words, hundreds of thousands of times. Only she hadn't had anyone to say them to. Just an empty bed and her own face in the mirror.

Now she had someone who was crazy about her, and she couldn't imagine why. But she wasn't above going with the flow for just a little longer. Until her fears overrode her passion for him, she supposed it was safe enough to see Jake. And when it got to the point that she had to face her abject terror, she would turn and run like hell and hope that it wouldn't take an eternity to tear Jake out of her heart.

HIS HEART WAS IN TOO BIG of a hurry, Jake told himself as he drove home. He was too anxious to know every part of Maggie, and it was frightening her away. He had seen her desire for him . . . there was no question about that. But he had also seen the dilemma in her eyes when she'd tried to make him understand why she couldn't—or wouldn't—sleep with him.

And it didn't take a genius to see her withdrawal back at her house. Maybe she was tired of him after they had spent the whole day together. Maybe taking her to meet his family had been a mistake. Maybe he was smothering her. Maybe she was losing interest.

He pulled into his driveway, killed the engine, sat for a moment, staring at the headlight shining on the back wall of the carport like the beginning of an idea taking shape in his brain. An idea he didn't much like, but one that had to be followed up on anyway.

He would have to give her space. That was all there was to it. Space had a way of healing burnout and fear. Tomorrow he wouldn't call her, and maybe not the next day, either. By the time he spoke to her again, maybe she would have figured out whether she really wanted to run away or continue seeing him.

It wasn't a good scenario, he had to admit, but it was better than the one in which she lost interest and started pushing him away. Maggie Conrad had a long way to go before she'd be rid of him.

Chapter Six

There was nothing wrong with her telephone. Maggie had verified that fact with the telephone company twice on Sunday and once on Monday. She had known that already, however, since the phone had rung twenty times for April and Steve. And it had worked fine when she'd called Jake and hung up on his answering machine.

Still, she hadn't heard from him since Saturday, and now, on Tuesday, as she sat in her philosophy class, trying desperately to concentrate, she was beginning to panic. Had he lost interest because she wouldn't sleep with him? Had she embarrassed him with his parents? Had he figured out that April was not her baby-sitter, but her baby?

The turmoil these thoughts had created within her, rendering her unable to think about her classes and her studies, making it impossible for her to focus on the dream she had waited so long for, was just one more sign. One that meant, as April had said, that the relationship was doomed. One that said Maggie shouldn't count on it any more than she had to. It was a sign that she was getting too attached to someone she should never have gotten involved with. It was a sign that she should keep her options open, so that when someone "right" came along, she would be available. It was a sign that she was on the losing side of a game she didn't understand. But she was learning fast.

"Miss Conrad? What are your thoughts on this?"

Maggie snapped her head up from her notes and focused on her professor—a tall, pensive man with kind, smiling eyes.

"Excuse me? Could you repeat the question?"

"I asked whether you found Plato's Cave to be comparable to any situation in today's life? Philosophy class, perhaps?"

Maggie smiled. Even though she'd had her thoughts centered on Jake for the past two days, she had managed to wade through her readings for today's class. "Not at all, Dr. Petri. I find philosophy class to be very stimulating. The office where I've worked for the last fifteen years reminds me a lot of Plato's Cave, though."

"Pity," her professor said. "There's nothing worse than wasting hour upon hour doing something that doesn't interest you."

"But until you've had a basis for comparison, you can't really know that, can you?" she asked.

His smile told her that he enjoyed her exchange immensely. "Yes, Miss Conrad. One always needs a basis for comparison. Plato's point exactly, I think."

Maggie sat back in her seat, chalking herself up one mental point for being able to hold her own with the professor. There had been a time, not so long ago, when she would have found it intimidating just to converse with someone like him. That she could not only do it now, but in front of twenty-two other classmates, told her she'd come a long way in a short amount of time. Part of her self-confidence she owed to Jake.

But she feared that when it was all over, she'd lose much more self-esteem than she'd had when she started.

A few minutes later, when Dr. Petri dismissed her class, Maggie took her time closing her books and stacking her folders. All morning she had lived in stark fear of not seeing Jake, but considering he'd ignored her for the past two days, she was even more afraid of actually running into him. What would she say? How would she act?

She wasn't adept enough at these games to know whether her face would reveal her despair. For that reason she found it best to steer clear of him until she had her heart better under control.

She had started out of the room when Dr. Petri touched her arm and stopped her. "Miss Conrad?"

"Yes."

"I wanted to tell you how much I enjoy your ideas. You're a very interesting woman."

"Me?" She gave a small, breathy laugh. "Well... thank you."

"I was wondering if—if it weren't too presumptuous of me... if perhaps I might ask you to dinner tonight."

"Dinner?" The word caught in her throat, and she felt her walls quickly snapping up. Her professor was asking her to dinner, and she hadn't even seen it coming!

"Uh...I don't know. I mean..." Her voice faltered and she thought of how desperately she'd hoped to hear from Jake tonight. A mental picture flashed into her mind of her sitting beside the phone, pretending to study while she waited for it to ring. The thought made her angrier at herself than at Jake. He had probably never meant to get her so involved. He'd had no idea how vulnerable she could be. To him, none of this was a big deal.

Which was exactly why she needed to go out with her professor. Pasting on her most charming smile, she said, "What I meant to say, Dr. Petri, is that I'd be honored to have dinner with you tonight."

"Splendid. And please, call me Eugene."

"All right, Eugene. You can call me Maggie."

"Maggie," he repeated. "It doesn't do you justice, you know. Still, it fits somehow."

She didn't know whether to thank him or be insulted, so she chose to do neither. Instead, she jotted her address on a piece of paper, handed it to him, and asked, "Seven all right?"

"Seven's perfect," he said, "although I don't relish the thought of waiting that long."

She smiled and started from the room. Turning at the door, she looked back at her professor, wishing he were a shade taller and that his hair was a little more unkempt and that he looked a little younger.... "I'll see you tonight," she said in a lackluster voice, then hurried out of the room.

As she dashed across campus to make her next class, Maggie considered whether it was another symptom of her insanity or sheer panic that had made her accept the invitation. She told herself that she needed that basis for comparison she'd so cleverly mentioned in his class. She needed to see what it could be like with someone her own age. It was time to ground her feet more firmly in reality.

BUT REALITY WAS A 1983 Chevrolet instead of a Harley-Davidson. Dinner at the neighborhood yuppy diner instead of a flight to Miami. And conversation about Plato's Cave rather than the time span for erupting passions.

The thought of passion never crossed her mind with Eugene—who Maggie would have preferred to continue calling Dr. Petri. In fact, the more she looked at him, the less desirable he became. His skin was too pale, and his hairline too receding. And every time he smiled, her eyes gravitated to the space between his front teeth.

"I feel sort of like a man in Plato's Cave sometimes," he was saying as he moved in closer to her at the secluded table he'd reserved for them. "When I saw you walk into my class, I saw that light he described. It was as if all the women I'd known before were mere shadows. And yet there I was, chained to the wall of the cave, only allowed to look at the silhouettes. I'd like to be released from those chains, Maggie."

Maggie looked at her watch and sighed. She wondered what Jake was doing tonight and if he'd tried to call while she was gone. She wondered if April would answer the phone and if she'd continue the charade of being the baby-sitter, or come clean once and for all. She wondered if the old headache routine would be too trite to use on Eugene. He'd probably heard it two hundred times. It was probably a typical ending to all of his dates.

"I know how you feel, Eugene," she said, trying to sound interested. "Chains, shadows. It's all so complicated. And yet, it's not." There, she thought. That ought to give him something to chew on for a while.

Anything to steer the conversation away from his bondage until he'd met her.

"What do you mean?"

She felt her stomach knotting tighter and wondered what to do now. "I just mean, things aren't always as they seem," she said, talking off the top of her head. Her genuinely aching head. "Old is young. Young is old. Wise is stupid..."

Suddenly, the idiocy in her words struck her as funny and she began to laugh. Eugene only stared at her, still trying to follow her profound wisdom.

"Please go ahead. I'm fascinated."

His interest only made her laugh harder and her eyes teared up. She clutched her side and bent over, desperately trying to curb her hysteria, but the harder she tried not to laugh, the more forceful it became. "It's just the whole thing... it's so disturbing, it's funny."

Eugene began to chuckle, too, and she was certain that was as hard as he'd laughed in years. "What, pray tell, is so funny?"

"Philosophy," she managed to squeak out. "If you think about it, it's so... so..."

"Pedantic?"

"Yes!" she almost shouted through her laughter. "Yes, that's exactly what I was going to say." The fact that she didn't even know what the word meant was even funnier to her, and she frantically searched through her purse for a tissue to wipe the tears now streaming down her face.

"I absolutely agree with you," Eugene said. "And yet, it's the stuff that adds a special spice to life. Not unlike your laughter."

She nodded agreement, and still tittering, said, "Not unlike motorcycles and spontaneous jaunts to Miami and making a living out of sand castles."

Eugene looked puzzled, but Maggie didn't care. Her laughter began to fade, and wiping her eyes again, she sighed. "Oh, Eugene. I haven't laughed like this in years."

"Nor I," he said. "And I really must thank you for it."

His response almost sent her into hysterics again as she pondered whether to let him in on the secret that she wasn't laughing *with* him, but at *him*. Feeling ashamed and trying to control herself, she slid her chair back. "I really need to get home, Eugene, but I have had a wonderful time."

"I hope you'll allow me another opportunity to bask in your light," he said. "You're a delightful person."

Maggie decided not to tell him just yet that she wouldn't have dinner with him again if she was starving in the street. Boredom was something she couldn't tolerate well. Not even for a free meal.

After he drove her home, she went inside and collapsed onto the couch, exhausted from the conversation, the culture and the hysteria that had taken her completely by surprise. The evening she had planned to get her mind off Jake had backfired. An older man, someone more suitable for her, had bored her to death. She had already been bitten by the May–December bug, and now she feared that no one could distract her from Jake.

"Mom?"

Maggie looked up to see her daughter dressed in a maternity nightgown, her bare feet peaking out from the bottom. "Hi, honey."

"You're home early," April said. "Didn't you have fun?"

"Loads. It was a night that I doubt could ever be repeated. At least, if I'm lucky."

"Jake called."

Maggie sprang to her feet. "He did? When? What did you tell him?"

"I lied for you again, Mom. I told him that you were out and that I was baby-sitting again. Which he wasn't too thrilled about. He wanted to know who you were out with."

"You didn't tell him, did you?"

"No, Mom. I lied and told him you were with Donald Trump. On his yacht. Trying on Marla's engagement ring."

"April, what did you really tell him?"

April shrugged. "I told him you were with some professor or something."

"Great. April, don't you know better than to tell one guy when I'm out with another?"

"I didn't know it was a mistake until I'd already done it," she said. "He was a little short after that, and I felt kinda sorry for him when he hung up."

"Really?" Maggie's spirits began to grow buoyant again. "You think he was jealous?"

"How should I know? I just know that he didn't like you being out with that professor guy."

"He's not the only one," Maggie said. She looked at the phone and wondered if it was still early enough to call Jake back. Would it give too much away?

"I'm going to make some popcorn for Steve," April said, heading into the kitchen. "But for what it's worth, Dr. What's-his-name is much more your type."

"How do you know what my type is, April?"

"Just my opinion," she said without apology as she disappeared through the door.

Maggie turned back to the phone, picked it up and, taking a deep breath, dialed Jake's number.

The answering machine answered, and this time Maggie hung on, hoping Jake was at home and just not answering.

"Jake? Are you there?" She paused long enough for him to pick up if he was home, but nothing happened. "This is Maggie. I'm sorry I missed your call, but I'm home now if you want to call back." Another pause. She racked her brain trying to decide whether to tell him she *really* wanted to talk to him, that she had missed him, that she couldn't sleep tonight until she heard his voice. But she waited too long, and the machine clicked off, and before she knew what had happened, the dial tone was humming in her ear.

ACROSS TOWN, Jake sat staring at his answering machine as if it were Maggie peeking in his window. He didn't even know why he hadn't picked up, but he told himself he really didn't want to talk to her.

How could she go out with some professor? The thought made him ill. He brought his gin and tonic to his lips and threw it back. She was supposed to be at home, worrying about why he hadn't called, missing him with every fiber of her being. She was supposed to be contemplating the space he'd given her and getting over her fears of him and the relationship that seemed to be moving so fast . . . and so deep.

But apparently it wasn't as deep as he'd thought. At least not on her part. Damn her! And damn that professor. And damn himself for letting a woman get this deep under his skin.

Getting up, Jake went back to the kitchen and poured another drink. But as he did, he realized it would take more than booze to get Maggie off his mind. He didn't actually know what it would take, but as he saw it, he had two choices: searching the world for the one thing that would exorcise her from his heart; or winning her for his own, once and for all. The latter sounded more appealing, so he sat down with his drink, staring at the wall and making a mental list of ways to win her back.

If it was a competition she wanted, he could play the game. And when he figured out his course of action, her professor wouldn't know what hit him!

THE PICTURE GREW MORE complicated the next afternoon when Maggie came home from work to find a bouquet of flowers that had been delivered while she was gone.

"They're pretty," April conceded, "but if they're from that guy you're robbing from the cradle, you ought to send them right back."

Maggie tore open the card and read the note aloud. " 'For the light you bring to the cave. Eugene.' "

"That professor guy?" April asked. "Mom, this is great! I don't even have to hide from him!"

"Yeah . . . great." Maggie dropped the card and started for her bedroom.

"Mom? Aren't you going to look at the flowers?"

Maggie shrugged. "I did. They're real pretty."

"But, Mom! How often have you gotten flowers from a man? Aren't you excited?"

"I got one from Jake the other day. He had a rose lying on my place mat."

"But this is a whole arrangement!"

Maggie turned around and set her hands on her hips. "April, remember that time you were sixteen and that guy, Jeremy, sent you a gift box of Chanel No 5 for Christmas? Do you remember how you felt?"

"I didn't want a gift from him," April said. "I didn't feel the same way about him...."

"Right."

April shook her head viciously, as if her mother couldn't possibly share that sentiment. "Mom, this isn't the same. I think what we have here is a case of your not seeing the forest for the trees."

Maggie squinted at her daughter and asked, "What trees?"

"Jake, that's what trees," April said, as if her point made absolute sense. "You've fallen for this guy who couldn't be more wrong for you, so you can't get interested in the other opportunities coming along. These flowers are a sign, Mom. A sign that you've got to keep your options open. When he loses interest because something younger has come along, you're going to need something to fall back on."

Maggie stared at April with dull eyes, then finally said, "I'm tired, April. I'm going to my room."

Before her daughter could beat her over the head with any more wisdom, Maggie went to her room, kicked off her shoes and collapsed on the bed.

Maybe it *was* a sign, she thought. Not a sign that Eugene was someone to be taken seriously—heaven knew she couldn't risk another date with him or he'd eventually realize the real source of her hysteria—but a sign that she was moving too fast into her feelings for Jake. It wasn't too late to pull back now. It wasn't too late to save herself from heartache.

Either that or her reaction to the flowers was a sign that she was too far gone already.

Whatever the sign meant, she couldn't wait to see Jake again, because if she didn't talk to him soon, she was afraid she'd show up at his door, ready to fulfill this relationship on his terms.

JAKE CALLED THE NEXT DAY, but the conversation was short and clipped. He didn't ask a thing about her professor, so Maggie didn't volunteer anything. And when he asked her if he could pick her up Saturday afternoon if he promised to have her back in time for dinner with "little April," Maggie had battled the disappointment that he hadn't asked to see her sooner and agreed.

The week was excruciating, and every time she saw him on campus, he seemed to be in a hurry. The only time she saw him consistently was after her philosophy class, and idly she wondered if he'd figured out that Eugene was the professor she'd dated. The thought gave her some small bit of satisfaction. If Jake was losing interest, he wouldn't care whom else she was seeing.

Saturday came at last, and Maggie fought the urge to throw her arms around Jake's neck when he arrived at her door. But when he took her into his arms, kissed her with the fever she had been battling all week, and whispered, "I don't remember ever suffering through a longer week," she felt herself melting and molding into whatever he needed her to be.

But Maggie got worried the minute Jake drove his Harley back into his driveway and cut the engine. Did he think he'd get her here and seduce her? Was he going to try romancing her again?

The week had been too tormenting, and she wasn't sure she could fight him off this time. Fight *him?* she thought with a mental grin. There wasn't any fighting to it. As frustrated as she'd been without touching him all week, she was afraid *he'd* have to fight *her* off. That was why she didn't want to go in.

But Jake seemed to sense her apprehension. "Don't worry, Maggie. My plans for this afternoon are outside."

"Outside?" she asked. "We're not going hang gliding or bungy jumping, are we?"

"No," he said with a laugh. "Something real simple. We're going to build the biggest, best sand castle you've ever seen."

"Really?" Her eyes lit up and she laughed aloud. "A real sand castle?"

"The kind that'll knock your socks off," he said. "And you have to realize that you're dealing with the best. I am the original Sand Man."

He took her hand then, and smiling, she let him lead her out into the sand.

FOUR HOURS LATER, Maggie sat back in the sand, which coated her legs up to her knees and her arms up to her elbows, and surveyed the wondrous creation she and Jake had worked on all afternoon.

"It's so beautiful," she said. "I want to live in it."

Jake laughed. "It would take me more than an afternoon to make it big enough to live in. A week, maybe."

Maggie sighed heavily. "But then the tide would rise and wash it all away."

"That's what happens, darlin'."

Jake leaned back next to her in the sand chairs he had made for them to view the beauty of their castle together and set his arm around her. It was all so simple, she thought. The waves shattering against the shore, the sea gulls cawing and dipping, the breeze blowing.

It was the best date she'd ever had, she realized. But it took a close second to both the night at the frat party and day in Miami. Smiling, she realized that every date with Jake was magic.

"What are you smiling about?" Jake asked, his voice a gentle rumble against her ear.

"Oh, nothing. Flower arrangements and sand castles. You."

"I've never sent you a flower arrangement."

Her smile grew broader. "I like sand castles better."

He leaned his head back on the sand headrest, and she leaned into him, resting her head on his shoulder. "I like sand castles, too," he said. "They have such a magical quality. They're so fragile and so temporary, but they're still worth every bit of the effort that goes into them."

Maggie's eyes misted over with the analogy to her relationship with Jake. It was fragile, temporary, but she was just now beginning to realize that it was worth every bit of heartache she was destined to suffer later.

"In the summer months, I come out here at 5:00 a.m.," he said, his voice still as soft and natural as the waves against the shore. "I start building sand walls around where I'm going to set up that day, and outside it, to draw attention, in the sand I make life-size mermaids and dolphins and alligators. And then I bring out my wares and my big umbrella with the words Sand Man printed on the edges, and by about nine, when the beachcombers start showing up, I'm in business."

"It sounds terrific," Maggie said. "Out here every day, with the music of the ocean and the sound of the gulls...."

"It gets old towards July. By August, I'm sick of it. I close on Labor Day every year." He sighed and looked out over the water, his eyes seeing bigger things than sand castles and mermaids. "I'm tired of sand," he said, not for the first time. "I want to have time for my serious art. I want to be known as Jake Abel, the artist, instead of Jake Abel, the Sand Man."

"There's nothing wrong with being a sand man," she said. "No one else could have made this castle for me today."

"No, it has its good points," he said. "And we all have to make a living. I have no real regrets. I just wish I could do more."

"Like that sculpture of Rachel?"

"Yeah." Jake smiled and touched Maggie's face with his thumb, running it along her cheekbone. "I'd like to do you. You have great bone structure in your face. And your eyes are so expressive. I just don't know if I could even come close to imitating what God did with you. And if you can't capture the spirit just right, it's almost a mockery to try."

Tears came to her eyes, and her mouth trembled as she whispered, "That's the sweetest thing anyone's ever said to me."

"Then you've been hanging around the wrong people," he whispered, and tipping her face gently up to his, he kissed her.

Maggie felt her heart pounding and her pulse bringing her whole body to life, and at that moment she had to admit she was falling faster than she'd ever imagined. She was falling in a way that was much more dangerous than hang gliding or bungy jumping.

She was falling in love.

JAKE WASN'T SURE what word to use to describe the way he was beginning to feel about Maggie, but he did know that it was nothing he'd ever felt before. It scared him to death, but at the same time, it became a sweet obsession. He found himself wandering through greeting-card stores, looking for poetic definitions for the gnawing in his heart, planning dream dates on his calendar for a whole month and listening to cry-in-your-beer country music for the first time in his life.

From where he sat, Maggie didn't seem as bothered by any such gnawing, however, and Jake noted that fact with growing chagrin. Although she seemed genuinely glad to hear from him each of the dozen times a day he called her—"just to hear your voice"—there was a decided lack of urgency in her desire to see him.

Her studies grew more burdensome since her course load was heavier than the average person could handle, and she took them more seriously than anyone he'd ever seen. Her dream of getting through school wasn't one she took lightly, and he had no doubt that her ardent dedication would help her to achieve far beyond her hopes. He just wanted to be around to see it.

She still wouldn't see him on weeknights, and weekends seemed to come with the same frequency as Christmas. But Maggie's bubbly smile when she met him at her door made the frustration he dealt with during the week almost worth it. They went dancing, shopping, saw movies through which she cried and he cuddled her, took long walks on the beach, and every time they came to the end of an evening, necking and kissing like teenagers, she always stopped it from going too far. He was going crazy, he admitted, but the craziest thing of all was that, for the first time in his life, he was falling for a woman emotionally and mentally before he'd even taken her clothes off.

It was a concept he'd never trusted before, but now he had to admit there was something to it.

But he couldn't fight the frustration he felt that her control was so much greater than his. And it haunted him that she never wanted him to come into her home when her daughter was home, and that she always made him drop her off at the curb. She didn't *seem* to be embarrassed by him—she never cowered from anyone they saw in public and there weren't places she shied away from. Maggie was willing to go anywhere with him and try anything, except for the one thing he'd had most on his mind. So why was she holding back so much?

He didn't know, but he made it his business to find out, and when they were coming on their fourth week of dating, their first month anniversary, Jake decided that he was going to break through at least one of the barriers. If it was the last thing he did, he would get closer to Maggie Conrad.

It took him a week to prepare for all the things he had planned for that night, and a full day of preparation at home. His anxiety was at its highest, but the greatest thought preying on his mind was that of making Maggie happy. He loved seeing her eyes light up, when he surprised her. He loved being responsible for that knock-'em-dead smile.

Tonight, that was his main goal. He grinned and thought that getting her into bed played a real close second.

THE JAZZ COMBO PLAYED a beautiful rendition of "Unforgettable," and Maggie looked around the restaurant in wonder and anticipated that the song was appropriate to the promise of tonight. Candlelight flickered on intimately placed tables, secluded by ficus trees and voluptuous ferns. But the poignant look in Jake's eyes was the most romantic part of the evening so far.

When he'd told her to wear her best dress, she had expected elegance, but when he'd shown up at her door wearing a tux and looking like one of those sexy male models from the pages of *Esquire,* her curiosity had launched a nervous fluttering in the pit of her stomach.

"I can't believe this," she said, feeling inexplicably awkward at the romantic mood he had set without pretense. "I've lived here all my life and I've never seen this restaurant."

His grin was maddening. "It's new. I had them open it just for you."

"You did not."

His laugh was soft and unconsciously seductive. "Well, I would have if I'd had the money. Especially tonight."

Her eyes sparkled as she brought her champagne to her lips. "Why tonight?"

Enjoying her confusion, Jake feigned disappointment. "You mean you don't remember?"

Maggie studied him for a moment, trying to remember. "Your birthday? You never told me! I'm sorry, Jake—"

His laughter cut into her apology. "No, not my birthday."

Maggie frowned. "Well, I know it's not mine. Is it a special holiday? Are you Jewish?"

"No, I'm not Jewish."

"Oh, I know. It's that equinox thing. When summer ends...?"

His laughter washed over the voices of the crowd. "I don't know if it is or not." He propped his chin on his hand, still grinning. "I can't believe you don't remember. You aren't the sentimental type, are you?"

"Well, usually, I am. Come on, Jake. What day is it?"

Laughing, he reached for her hand and brought it to his lips. Then fixing his gaze on her wide eyes, he whispered, "It's our first-month anniversary, darlin'."

"Really? A whole month?" It pleased her that he would remember something so obscure—something even she hadn't made note of. She'd rarely known a man who kept up with such things.

"Four weeks of bliss," he said, his eyes holding her in an unyielding embrace. "The best...and longest...four weeks of my life."

Maggie looked down at her place setting and ran her finger along the silver spoon. "Longest?"

"Yes," he whispered. "It's the longest I've ever dated anyone without spending the night with her."

Maggie felt her face flush with a heat to rival the candlelight and she hid her expression behind her wineglass. "Well, I guess by now you know I'm not just anyone."

"You're telling me," he said, and she saw the seriousness in his eyes.

She sat staring at him, mesmerized by his hypnotic gaze. His smile reached his eyes before it made its way to his lips. "Eat your escargot, darlin'. It's getting cold."

Sighing, Maggie smiled and picked up the tiny fork and reached into one of the shells. But instead of the snail delicacy she expected to find, her fork pulled out something else.

"What's this?" Withdrawing the fork, she saw a tiny gold chain unfolding from its hiding place.

"Gosh, I don't know," Jake said, a decidedly guilty grin on his face.

She pulled the chain farther out and saw the tiny white seashell attached it. "Oh, Jake. Did you do this?"

"No way," he said. "I think the chef must just have a mad crush on you. Who can blame him?"

She smiled, then started to clasp the chain behind her neck, but Jake scooted his chair back and came to his feet. "Here, let me help you put it on."

Maggie looked up at him as he draped the chain around her neck. He bent down to her ear and whispered, "It reminds me of that day in Miami when we were looking for driftwood and you kept finding shells you wanted to keep. This looks like one of them. Wonder how the chef got it."

As Jake was leaning over her, Maggie kissed his cheek. "Jake, this is so sweet. But I didn't get you anything. I didn't know..."

"As the song says, tie a bow around yourself, dar-lin'," he whispered, and cupping her chin in his hand, he brought her face to his and kissed her gently.

"Excuse me, sir."

Startled, they both looked up to see the grinning waiter. "May I take your plates?"

"Sure," Maggie said, relinquishing her escargot dish to him and shooing Jake back to his chair.

"I didn't mean to disturb anything," the waiter said. "It looks like a special night for the two of you."

Maggie smiled. "It's our anniversary."

"Oh? And how many years have you been married?"

Jake set his hand over Maggie's and said, "Five."

Maggie snapped her amused eyes at him. "What?"

"Haven't we been married five years, darlin'?"

Maggie glanced up at the waiter, who had almost finished setting the table. "Well...yes. It's just that he always gets it wrong. I was surprised he remembered for once."

"Nag, nag, nag," Jake said, a soft, laughing rum-ble on his voice. He brought her hand to his lips again and kissed it, negating his words.

"Enjoy your meal," the waiter said.

Jake picked up the breadbasket and passed it to Maggie. She pulled back the napkin and reached in for the bread, but instead she came out with a small gold box with a bow tied around it. "What is this?"

Again Jake's eyes danced with amusement. "Darn that chef. I might have to go have a talk with him."

Not fooled for a moment, Maggie took in a deep, shaky breath. "Jake, you shouldn't have done all this."

"I had nothing to do with it. Just open it."

She took off the bow, grinning like a little girl at her own birthday party. "I feel like I should make a wish," she said.

He laughed softly. "No, darlin'. The gifts are for you, but the wishes are all mine."

Her eyes grew smoky as she met his gaze. "And what wishes are those?"

His smile was mesmerizingly sensual. "Just open the gift."

She tore off the paper, uncovering a small crystal paperweight. "I love it," she said. "I've never had anything like this before."

He propped his chin on his hand. "When I looked into it, I saw everything about you." His voice dropped to a subtle, teasing note. "I saw your darkest secrets, your deepest anxieties, your greatest desires...."

She laughed and tried to see into the crystal herself. "All that and you're still taking me out? Let's see. What can I see about you?"

"Uh-oh." He leaned over the table, as if reading the crystal with her.

"Ooh," she said, shaking her head. "There you are, scratching your head with confusion, wondering how you got involved with someone like me. Uh-oh, here comes a good-looking blonde in a bikini, and suddenly you're coming to your senses...."

"Give me that." Jake grabbed the crystal out of her hand. "This thing doesn't work. I'm taking it back!" Laughing, Maggie took the crystal back and held it to her heart. "All right, I confess. I didn't really see that."

"Whew," Jake said with a grin. "I thought I'd gotten hold of a defective crystal. The future I see there is much, much different."

Her eyes darted up to his and her smile faded. "What future?" she asked quietly.

He smiled. "Yours, mine. Tonight, tomorrow, next week."

Her eyes were shining as she looked at him, and he whispered, "Drink your champagne."

Dinner was hazed in magic and wonderment, and Maggie knew that as long as she lived, no one would ever be able to follow this act. It would be hopeless to find anyone who measured up to Jake. The thought almost saddened her, but she fought it off, telling herself that it was now that mattered. Not tomorrow. Not next week. Not the day that Jake left her for a younger, more attractive woman.

She could barely eat the meal that had been so carefully, so expertly prepared, but when the waiter returned to the table, Jake insisted on dessert, anyway. He ordered a chocolate soufflé that she knew he'd had to order far in advance, so she made up her mind to do her best to eat it, if the fluttering in her stomach allowed it.

"You take the first bite," he said, handing her the fork. "And reach deep. The good stuff's at the bottom."

She took the utensil and scooped a bite, but Jake caught her hand. "Deeper, darlin'," he whispered. "It's best when you go deep."

The room felt suddenly hot, and Maggie wondered if everyone else in the restaurant felt it, too. She knew her face was growing crimson, and she felt a throbbing in her core from an undeniable hunger that no food could satiate. Finally she had to admit that she was growing weary with dinner, for she wanted nothing more right now than to go home with Jake, feel his arms around her and see what happened if just this once, she let nature take its course.

She thrust the fork deeper and at once realized why Jake had been so insistent. There was another box at the bottom of the soufflé. A smile crept across her face as she tried to scoop it out. "Jake, not another one."

"You mean he did it again?" Jake asked with a grin. "Looks like the chef and I are going to have to step outside and settle this."

She wiped off the chocolate and saw that the gift-wrapped box was enveloped inside a little plastic bag. Opening it, she withdrew the box. "Jake, I can't believe you went to all this trouble. It's the sweetest thing anyone's ever—"

He set his finger on her lips to hush her, and said, "See what it is."

She tore open the box and took out a tiny gold object. "A compass?"

"To help you find your way around campus," he said. "But this is a special compass. No matter where you go, it'll always bring you back to me."

She moved the compass around and saw that he was serious. No matter where she held it, it always pointed to Jake. "Do you have a magnet vest on or something?"

He moved his face maddeningly close to her ear and, stroking her neck with the tips of his fingers, whispered, "When we get home, you can find out. But you have to look real carefully. If it's there, it's hidden away. You might have to take off everything I'm wearing to find it."

She knew her cheeks were again reddening in mottled patches, but instead of withdrawing, she found herself nuzzling his face, closing her eyes and pictur-

ing the scene he described for her. Taking off his tie, his
coat, his shirt, his pants...

Quickly she pulled herself away and reached for her
champagne. Trying to steady her breathing, she
brought the glass to her lips. Something in the bottom
of the crystal glass moved, then floated around again.
She looked through the side and saw the tiny key
floating in the bubbly liquid. "Jake, there's something in there."

"Well get it out."

Not sure if it was the champagne or the situation,
Maggie started to giggle as she reached in and fished
out the key. Setting it in her palm, she asked, "What
is this?"

He set his napkin down and moved his face closer to
hers. "The key to my heart."

If any other man had said it at any other time, Maggie would have burst out laughing. But coming from
Jake at this moment, the words brought tears to her
eyes. One broke free and dropped over her lashes, and
she leaned across the corner of the table and set her wet
hand on his cheek. "You are the sweetest, most
thoughtful man I've ever met."

He touched her chin and brought her closer, and this
time his kiss was deep and urgent, almost desperate.
Heat rose up from Maggie's core and spread through
her bloodstream, palpitating heat, throbbing heat,
desperate heat...

Smoky heat.

She pulled back as she smelled the smoke wafting
across the air and glanced around.

"Fire!" someone across the room shouted.

"Oh, my God!" Maggie threw her hands over her face as she realized that the flames in question were at *their* table. Tall flames, dancing flames, hot flames.

Jake dumped his water glass on the fire, but it wasn't enough, so one of the fellow diners dashed across the room, and, with his napkin, began beating out the flames. The dish with packs of sugar had gone up in a small conflagration of its own, and Jake knocked it to the floor and began stomping out the blaze.

Before anyone had the chance to react, the sprinkler system sprang into action, and a dozen showers sprayed throughout the room. Diners left their seats, running, arms draped over their heads as if that would protect them from the torrent of water.

Maggie only sat still in her seat, letting the water pour down on her, and with both hands covering her mouth, she gave in to the hysteria that had been flanking her all night.

Jake reached for her hand and tried to pull her from her seat. "Come on, let's get out of here."

She rose to her feet, but instead of running, threw her arms around his neck. He was soaked from head to toe, and so was she, but that didn't change anything about the way she felt. "You are an amazing man," she said, laughter still rolling on her voice as the sprinklers rained down upon them. "And I'll never forget this night as long as I live."

"Neither will anyone else who was here," Jake said. He kissed her then, crushing her wet body against him, but laughter still punctuated their kiss.

"Let's get out of here," he said, "before the fire department blows us out with their hoses."

Clutching her stomach with laughter, Maggie reached for all of her presents, then took Jake's arm.

Before they left, he turned back to the table, grabbed the champagne bottle, then said, "Let's go."

The maître d' was waiting just outside the door when they left, and informed them that all of tonight's dinners were on the house because of the fire. Before they started out to the car, the man caught Maggie's arms. "Miss, I really feel I must tell you this in case you don't already know."

Still giggling, Maggie asked, "What?"

"Anytime your table catches on fire and your date doesn't notice, that's the ultimate compliment."

Gales of laughter rose from both Jake and Maggie, and stumbling against each other, they made their way, dripping, to her car.

THERE WAS NO CHOICE but to change out of the clothes they had worn, so when they reached the beach house, Jake changed into a pair of red jogging shorts and gave Maggie a long T-shirt that hung almost to her knees. When she came out of the bathroom, obviously braless, he felt something in his groin tighten. He wondered if she'd taken off her panties, as well, for he knew that he had been soaked clear through to his skin.

The thought of her naked body beneath that shirt distracted him madly, but the self-conscious, almost shy look on her face told him not to act on the impulse to pull her against him and slide his hands under the shirt just to see. Because if she let him do that and he did find her naked, he wouldn't be able to control what happened after that. And if it was the last act of grace he had to offer, Jake was going to wait to make love to her until she wanted it as much as he did.

But he couldn't speak as he beheld her; something seemed to have caught in his throat. He was smotheringly hot, and he thought that if she wasn't ready to be intimate just yet, he would have to get out where he could breathe.

The moon was full over the Gulf, and Jake opened the sliding doors to his living room, letting the smell of sea breeze and salt air fill his dwelling. He took two glasses from his kitchen, the bottle of champagne and Maggie's hand. He pulled her out onto the deck, down the steps and out across the sand.

"It's beautiful," she said, her voice a breathy whisper. "As long as I live, Jake, I will never forget this night. No man's ever tried to burn a restaurant down for me."

Chuckling, Jake grabbed the blanket he kept draped on his deck and spread it out on the sand. He dropped onto the blanket and pulled her down beside him. "And you're worth every spark in that raging fire," he whispered. "I'm crazy about you. You know that, don't you?"

He slid his arms around her as he spoke, and she gazed up into his eyes, eyes that were smoky with desire, eyes that made her melt and sizzle. "Why?" she asked.

"Because you're beautiful," he whispered, kissing her neck. "Because you're intelligent." His kiss rose to her ear, and she shivered as his tongue dipped inside. "Because you're different." His voice was a maddening breath in her ear.

She turned her face to his and caught his lips in a devouring kiss, a kiss that robbed her of all sanity. He lowered her back to the blanket and stretched out beside her, deepening the kiss. He felt her breasts crushing across his bare chest in a maddening display of her desire, felt her nipples peaking through the jersey knit.

His hand roved over her breast through the cloth, touching, molding, caressing, until she arched her back and moaned softly. He touched her bare knee, moved his hand up the smooth flesh of her thigh. When Maggie didn't stop him, he moved higher, until her bare hip was hot against his palm. Then he felt the damp scrap of panties she still wore, and he knew that his sanity was straddling the edge of control.

His hand moved upward to the bare, full mound of her breast. He started to raise the T-shirt, but her hand caught the hem and stopped him. Not giving her the chance to voice her objection, Jake caught her breast with his mouth through the T-shirt, suckling her sharp nipple in spite of the cloth, the wetness of his tongue leaving a hunger-crazed ring around her aureola.

She shuddered and arched her back as he suckled first one breast and then the other, licking and biting and caressing with his tongue.

Her breath came in short gasps, and his hand moved lower. Maggie stopped his hand and moved it to her back, still unable to commit to the seduction she was falling prey to, the seduction she had dreamed about, the seduction she wanted to return.

Jake claimed her mouth again, his tongue playing sensual games with hers as he moved above her, settling against her in an aching nonunion that only teased and tempted and tested. She felt the extent of his desire for her through his red jogging shorts, and knew at once that he'd worn no underwear beneath the silky scrap of fabric. Tiny firework explosions shot from her core, making her want more than anything to shed her panties and that huge T-shirt and give herself to him right here on the sand.

NO RISK, NO OBLIGATION TO BUY...NOW OR EVER!

CASINO JUBILEE
"Scratch'n Match" Game

Here's how to play:

1. Peel off label from front cover. Place it in space provided at right. With a coin, carefully scratch off the silver box. This makes you eligible to receive two or more free books, and possibly other gifts, depending upon what is revealed beneath the scratch-off area.

2. You'll receive brand-new Harlequin American Romance® novels. When you return this card, we'll rush you the books and gifts you qualify for, ABSOLUTELY FREE!

3. If we don't hear from you, every month we'll send you 4 additional novels to read and enjoy months before they are available in bookstores. You can return them and owe nothing, but if you decide to keep them, you'll pay only $2.96* per book, a saving of 43¢ each off the cover price. There is **no** extra charge for postage and handling. There are **no** hidden extras.

4. When you join the Harlequin Reader Service®, you'll get our subscribers-only newsletter, as well as additional free gifts from time to time, just for being a subscriber!

5. You must be completely satisfied. You may cancel at any time simply by sending us a note or a shipping statement marked ''cancel'' or by returning any shipment to us at our cost.

YOURS FREE!

This lovely heart-shaped box is richly detailed with cut-glass decorations, perfect for holding a precious memento or keepsake—and it's yours absolutely free when you accept our no-risk offer.

CASINO JUBILEE
"Scratch'n Match" Game

CHECK CLAIM CHART BELOW
FOR YOUR FREE GIFTS!

YES! I have placed my label from the front cover in the space provided above and scratched off the silver box. Please send me all the gifts for which I qualify. I understand I am under no obligation to purchase any books, as explained on the opposite page.

(U-H-AR-09/92) 154 CIH AFPD

Name _____

Address _____ Apt. _____

City _____ State _____ Zip _____

◀ DETACH AND MAIL CARD TODAY! ▶

◄ DETACH AND MAIL CARD TODAY! ◄

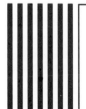

NO POSTAGE
NECESSARY
IF MAILED
IN THE
UNITED STATES

BUSINESS REPLY MAIL
FIRST CLASS MAIL   PERMIT NO. 717   BUFFALO, NY

POSTAGE WILL BE PAID BY ADDRESSEE

HARLEQUIN READER SERVICE
3010 WALDEN AVE
PO BOX 1867
BUFFALO NY 14240-9952

But fear debilitated her, rendering her unable to follow her heart.

"Let's go inside," he whispered against her lips, his voice nothing more than a wisp of sound that competed with the waves lapping against the shore.

"No," she whispered, her voice trembling like her body. "I can't."

"Maggie, I want you. I think about you every hour of the day. You're driving me crazy."

"It's not that I don't want you, too. It's just . . ."

He waited, but she never finished her thought. "Just what?"

"Just . . ."

He sat up, gazing down at her with more patience in his eyes than she would have expected. His voice still trembled when he spoke. "Maggie, talk to me. Is it me?"

"No," she said, tears springing to her eyes. "It's me. I'm scared."

"Scared of me?" he asked. "Don't you know by now that you don't have to be scared of me?"

"Not *of* you," she whispered. "I'm scared of how you'll feel afterward. I'm a lot older than you, Jake. The other women you've gone out with are so young."

"Is that it? The age thing?"

She wiped her eyes and looked out over the water. "Maybe a little."

"All right," he said, facing her. "Let's get this over with. How old *are* you?"

Her face felt as hot as simmering coals, and she swallowed, only to discover that her mouth had gone dry.

"Come on, Maggie. If we're gonna move this relationship forward, which I intend to do, we have to get past this."

Maggie looked down at the sand and traced a finger pattern through it. "I'm thirty...ish."

He grinned. "Thirtyish? What does that mean?"

"Forty, all right? It means forty!" She sprang to her feet and took off across the sand. "Are you happy, Jake? Does that make you feel any better? Or do you want to turn and run as fast as you can?"

Jake caught her and wrestled her around to him. He took her hands, but she pulled them away and he started to laugh. "Maggie, I practically burned a building down for you tonight. The least you can do is talk to me."

"How can I talk to you about this when you're laughing at me?" she asked. "This isn't funny!"

"I'm not laughing about your age, darlin'," he said, still chuckling. "I'm laughing about your absolute certainty that it makes any difference at all. That's crazy, Maggie. I don't care how old you are."

He took her hands again and pulled her against him, still laughing. "And I'm laughing about those little wrinkles around your eyes when you're upset."

"Terrific," she said. "First you beat my age out of me, and then you insult my face."

"I'm not insulting your face," he said, touching it with a sacred reverence that no one had ever shown her before. "I love your face. It's the most beautiful face I've ever seen. And I love your hair."

"It's gray, you know. When you look at it in the light, it glistens with gray."

Again he laughed. "People pay to have their hair frosted like that." He kissed her and slid his hand down to trace the soft shape of her breast. A sigh escaped his lips as he feathered a fingertip over the wet ring where he'd suckled. "In fact, I love your whole body. Especially your breasts." His hands cupped and massaged over them again, and he looked down at them, his eyes glistening with desire. "Tell me something, Maggie. If I wasn't absolutely bowled over by your body, would I have this much of an obsession with your breasts?"

"You haven't *seen* my whole body," she whispered.

"Not for lack of trying," he pointed out as he nibbled at her bottom lip. "But I like the way it feels...." His hand massaged that breast again, making Maggie whimper and arch her head back. He dipped his face to her neck, nuzzled it, then lowered to her breast again and took it in his mouth.

When her moan reached her throat, he took her mouth again. His kiss this time was deeper, more demanding, and Maggie felt herself slipping away, unable to turn back.

He bent down, whisked her up in his arms and carried her back to the blanket. "I'm going to make love to you now, Maggie," he whispered, his voice rough and shaky as he laid her down. "Because if I don't I'm gonna lose my mind."

Her mind struggled for some bearing, but his hand still moved over her, making her tremble and shudder and shiver. And before she knew what kind of consent it would mean, she pulled him into a desperate kiss.

His hands moved wildly over her now, and, in one reckless motion, slipped her panties down her thighs. He filled his hands with her buttocks, then pulled her shirt over her head and caught one bare nipple in his mouth.

Her body screamed with tormented excitement as
Jake worked his magic over her, and when he pulled
out of his own shorts, her heart galloped out of control.

She basked in the luxury of her breasts against his
chest, and when he slid over her and consummated the
union she had avoided for so long, a bright ecstasy shot
through her, coupled with a raging relief.

Afterward, laying naked in the moonlight, the breeze
whispering over her skin, her head on his chest, their
legs entangled, Maggie listened to the sound of Jake's
heartbeat slowing from marathon speed to that of rest.

Jake kissed the top of her head. "You're beautiful,
Maggie," he whispered. "And soon I'm going to make
love to you in the light and prove it to you."

She looked up at him with love in her eyes and wondered if he realized how much what had just happened
bonded her to him. Did he feel connected to her now,
or was it just a physical act to him? Did he know that
letting go of him after tonight would devastate her? Did
he feel the same way?

They fell into a deep sleep, as if they could only relax their fullest in each other's arms.

It was 3:00 a.m. when Maggie woke, chilled by the
sudden drop in temperature and the sound of the waves
beating against the shore. She insisted that Jake take
her home so that her daughter wouldn't think exactly
what had happened had happened, and so she could
"relieve" the fictitious baby-sitter he thought was
there.

Smiling sleepily, Jake drove her home in her car, and
before he got onto his Harley to ride it home, he
cupped Maggie's chin. "Don't forget what the man
said, darlin'. The restaurant was burning down around

me and I didn't even notice. That's what you do to me.''

Then giving her one last kiss, he opened her front door. ''Good night, darlin'. Get plenty of rest. You're an addiction now, and you're going to need lots of energy from now on.''

A wry grin stole across her mouth as he ambled back to the motorcycle, chuckling all the way.

Chapter Seven

"Mom, are you awake? Mom?"

April's voice cut into the depths of her sleep, and Maggie cracked open an eye and moaned something incoherent.

"Mom, it's ten o'clock! You never sleep this late!"

Maggie lifted her head off the pillow and squinted up at her daughter. "I'm allowed to sleep in on a Saturday if I want to, April. I'm tired."

"That's what you get for gallivanting around till all hours of the night," April shot back, sitting on the edge of the bed. "But this is important."

"What?" Maggie asked, forcing herself to sit up. "It better be good."

"Can Steve borrow your car?"

"For what?"

"For his new job. It's just temporary, but he's going to be a cashier at the theater until something better comes along. He got hired last night. We were standing in line at the movies when the manager fired one of the cashiers for cursing at a customer. Next thing I know, my husband marches right up to him and asks for the job. And you thought he wasn't worth anything. Wow, talk about being in the right place at the right time.''

''Gee,'' Maggie said, rubbing her head and wondering if the headache she felt was from a hormone overload last night or too much champagne. ''I always said he was a genius with timing.''

April recognized the barb for what it was and bristled. ''Mother, he's doing the best he can. Can he borrow your car or not?''

Maggie nodded and shoved her hair back from her face. ''All right, April. I guess so.''

''Thanks, Mom.'' April leaned over and gave her mother a kiss. ''Oh, and do we have any Pepto-Bismol? I've had killer indigestion this morning.''

''Look in the medicine cabinet in my bathroom.''

April disappeared, and Maggie slid out of bed and looked at herself in the mirror. Something stared back at her, something that resembled a witch that had just wrestled an orangutan. And the ape had won.

Had she looked like that when she woke and made Jake take her home? Oh, Lord, she thought. He must be so repulsed.

She'd be lucky if she ever saw him again. He'd probably run when he saw her coming on campus. Feeling sick, as if she'd just destroyed her life in one fell swoop, she ran to the bathroom, bent over the sink and splashed cold water into her face.

''You look awful.''

She turned around and saw April standing at the open medicine cabinet, sipping Pepto-Bismol as if it were a soft drink. ''Thanks, honey. I appreciate that.''

''I'm telling you, dating younger men will wear you out.''

''Oh? And what do you know about it?''

"I just know that I've never seen you keep such long hours in my whole life. Sooner or later, he's going to wear you out."

April sashayed out of the bathroom, preceded by her stomach, and left Maggie alone with that horrid image.

"All right," Maggie said, lifting her chin and refusing to be done in by a mere reflection. "Even Brooke Shields probably looks like hell when she wakes up. I'll bet Julia Roberts has huge bags under her eyes. I'll bet her hair looks like a rat's nest and her breath would kill a goat."

The thought made Maggie feel better, and quickly she began applying her makeup. Slowly the witch began to disappear and some semblance of her old self emerged. When she had finished, she gazed into the mirror again. "All right, see? All women look like hags first thing in the morning. Even the ones who look great in bikinis. It's only temporary."

But that realization didn't do a thing to lessen her anxiety. She and Jake had crossed the line from dates to lovers last night. And she wasn't fool enough to believe it was the only time it would happen. Once it did, it was hard to stop. Impossible, even.

And one of those times, she wouldn't wake at three, but at six or seven, when the sun was out, and she wouldn't be able to hide in the dark. One of those times he'd see what a wreck she was in the morning.

Maggie went back to her bed, plopped down on it and told herself it was hopeless. She had sealed her fate last night and now all she could do was wait for the bomb to drop. She would be the one to get hurt, and that was the last thing she needed right now.

Oh, why hadn't she just buried herself in her studies and pretended that she'd never met Jake Abel? Despite what he'd said last night, he'd probably gotten it out of his system now that his curiosity had been sated after finding out there was nothing special about her, except that she had a lot more miles on her old bod than most of the women he knew. Today he was probably riding his Harley with some freshman in a thong bikini.

She heard an engine in the driveway and assumed it was Steve in her car. But from the living room, April called, "Mom, Jake's here!"

"Jake?" Maggie called as her heart dropped to her feet. "Oh, no! I'm not dressed."

"I'll let him in!" April called.

"Okay," Maggie said, rushing to the closet and grabbing a pair of jeans and a T-shirt. Then suddenly, she realized what she had just agreed to. Jake would see April in her robe and realize that she lived here....

Dashing to the door, she screamed, "No! Don't answer it!"

But it was too late. April had already opened the door and Jake was gaping down at her.

Maggie fell back into her bedroom. Fighting the despair welling up inside her, she began tugging on her jeans. Then sliding on her bra and her T-shirt and ignoring her hair, she rushed out of the bedroom.

"Jake, what are you doing here?"

He looked up from April, then his eyes gravitated back to her. "I just thought I'd surprise you," he said. "But it looks like I'm the one who's surprised."

April turned around, still holding the Pepto-Bismol and sporting a thin, pink mustache. "I'm sorry, Mom. I forgot."

"Mom?" Jake uttered a humorless laugh, but Maggie could hear the anger wavering just beneath the surface of his tone. "So she's really your daughter? You've been lying to me?"

"Jake, I wanted to tell you, but I was afraid you'd think—"

Before she could finish, Steve bopped into the room and began digging into her purse for her keys. "Hey, man, how's it goin'?" he said to Jake.

"Jake," Maggie began, even more apprehensive than before. "You've met my son-in-law, Steve."

"Do we have to hide outside this time, Maggie?" Steve asked cheerfully.

Jake didn't find it amusing. "So everyone was in on the joke? You mind telling me why you had to go to all this trouble just to pull one over on me?"

Steve flashed a grin and a shrug that said it wasn't his problem. "Come walk me to the car, babe. I'm outta here." Then to Jake, he said, "You guys try not to break anything if the fists start flying."

Maggie shot him a killer glare as April followed him out, still sipping Pepto-Bismol. But before Steve left the house, he shouted, "See you later, Grandma."

Maggie's heart crashed like a water balloon dropped from a thirteen-story building. She turned back to Jake, who still stood at the door, gaping.

"Jake?"

His gaze was lethal when he brought it back to her. "Why did you keep this from me? Why did you make me believe she was just a kid?"

"She *is* just a kid. A pregnant, married kid. And I didn't want you to know, because I knew it would make me seem even older—"

"Maggie, give me a break! We've been seeing each other a month, and I didn't even know one of the most important things about your family! What else have you lied to me about?"

The back door closed as April came back in. They heard the car pulling away.

"It wasn't a *malicious* lie," Maggie whispered. "Just a little white one. All right, several little white ones. Admit it, Jake. You wouldn't have kept seeing me if you'd known I was about to be somebody's grandmother!"

"Maggie, I told you last night that my feelings for you have absolutely zilch to do with your age. But that's not the point. I don't like being lied to. I thought we were building some trust between us."

"We were... we are. But I just wanted to enjoy it a little longer before it had to blow up in my face."

"Blow up in your face?" he shouted. "Damn it, Maggie, I really appreciate your confidence in what we've got going here. What do you think? I just spend all this time with you for the challenge?"

Maggie glanced toward the kitchen, self-conscious about being overheard, and she lowered her voice. "Well, that could be. After last night, you might have been ready to give me the ax—"

He grabbed her shoulders and shook her, his eyes flaming as he fixed them on her. "Damn it, Maggie!" He dropped his voice to a vicious whisper. "The only disappointment I had last night was that I couldn't hold you all night long and wake up with you in my bed. Does that sound like the kind of feeling that's going to blow up in your face?"

"No, Jake," she said, tears bursting into her eyes. "No, it doesn't."

"Then why did you lie?"

"I was confused," she said. "And stupid. I wasn't thinking. I was just scared. I've never had anything like this before, and I didn't want to take the chance of losing it."

"But you had plans for it to end, didn't you? Otherwise, you wouldn't have used such a temporary lie. You had to know I'd find out eventually."

She couldn't meet his gaze when she answered. "I thought by then we'd be out of each other's systems and that you'd be long gone."

"Long gone," he said through his teeth. "You've expected me to evaporate since the first day you met me, haven't you? That's why you've been building up your stable of alternate dates. Or maybe *I'm* the alternate."

Maggie gaped at him. "What are you talking about?"

"I'm talking about your professor friend and God knows who else."

"Jake, I only went out with him once, and I only did it because—"

"It doesn't matter, Maggie. All I want to know is if you lied to him, too."

"Jake . . . there was no need—"

"No, I didn't think so," he bit out. "The joke's just on me, isn't it, Maggie? I'm just a part of some grand hoax by you and your family."

He reached for the door, but Maggie tried to stop him. "Jake, don't go."

"You lied to me, Maggie," he said again, hurt climbing like flames in his eyes. "I hate lies. Women who lie to me don't often get a second chance." He ran his shaking fingers through his hair and flung the door open.

"But those other women didn't have reasons like I have, Jake!" she said, fighting her tears with all her might. "Damn it, you don't know what it's like to have a dream and have a dozen obstacles to fulfilling it. You don't know what it's like to climb a ladder when all the rungs keep breaking beneath your weight."

"You're making straight A's in school, Maggie, so don't tell me the rungs keep breaking. You're fulfilling your dream better than I am."

"I'm not talking about that dream, Jake," she cried. "I'm talking about my new dream. The one where I risk enough to fall in love again, where I crawl far enough out on a limb to trust again, where I take the ultimate act of faith and believe in someone again."

"I believed, too, Maggie," Jake said through his teeth. "But I'm the one who was lied to, remember?"

Maggie stood gaping at him as he turned and strode across the lawn to his bike. For a moment, she struggled between the urge to drop to the floor in a wilted, defeated heap and the urge to run after him and beg him not to leave.

Tears burst from her eyes and streamed down her cheeks, and her hands shook as she stood paralyzed, staring at the door.

Outside on his bike, Jake jerked his helmet on, snapped the chin strap and cranked the engine. It revved beneath him with more power than he'd ever need, but it still did nothing to match the anger swelling in his heart.

But battling that anger was that emotion he had only recently been able to confront. That emotion that had made him wake much earlier than he should have today and yearn to have his arms around Maggie again. That emotion that had branded her name on his heart, no matter what other emotion tried to smother it out. That emotion that told him that if he rode away now, he'd be confirming every fear that had kept her holding back for so long.

Damn her! Why had she lied to him about something so important? Why had she had so little faith in him that she could believe the age of her daughter made any difference at all? Was this a battle he'd have to fight for the rest of his life?

He looked up the street in the direction he should be riding and told himself that it didn't matter if it was. Even a lifelong battle to convince her of the inconvincible was preferable to living without her. Even choking back his anger long enough to tell her that he'd be back, that he just needed to vent somewhere alone, that they'd talk about this later was better than risking losing her.

Frustrated, he turned off the engine, dragged off his helmet, and went back to the door.

Maggie was still standing where he'd left her, and when she saw him, she slapped at her tears and stared up at him. "I thought you were leaving," she said defiantly.

Again that anger swirled up inside him. "Damn it, Maggie, I want to. But before I go, I want you to know that I'm just gonna find something to ram my fist through, and after I get my hand bandaged up, I'll be back."

A reluctant smile broke through her tears, and Maggie breathed a soft laugh. "Okay."

He sighed heavily and backed out the door, but before he was completely gone, they heard a crash in the kitchen. Maggie swung around. "April?"

April's voice was strangled when she cried, "Mom! Help!"

Maggie dashed into the kitchen, Jake following behind her, and saw her daughter kneeling in a puddle of water. "Oh, my God. Her water's broken."

"Mom, I think the baby's coming!"

"No, it can't!" Maggie cried, running to the window. "Steve took the car!"

"We can take her on the Harley," Jake offered weakly.

April clutched her stomach and muffled a scream. "Oh, Mom, it hurts! I feel that pressure that I'm not supposed to feel till the end."

"Oh, God!" Maggie ran to the phone, handed it to Jake, and cried, "Call the doctor. Call an ambulance. Call 911."

"Which one?" he asked.

"911!" Maggie cried. "Hurry!"

She tried to pull April to her feet, but the girl doubled over again. "Oh, Mom, there's no time," she screamed. "It's coming!"

"Breathe!" Maggie cried, trying to remember some of the breathing techniques she'd used so long ago— before she had demanded anesthesia at the threat of assassinating the doctor. "Come on, *breathe!*"

"I . . . can't!" April screamed. "Mom, help me!"

Jake hung up the phone and ran into the living room to grab a pillow off the couch, yelling behind him as he went. "The ambulance is on the way. We just have to make her comfortable until it gets here."

"Oh, right," April grunted through her teeth as Maggie forced her to lie on the floor. "I feel real comfortable, all right." Another contraction seized her, and she cried, "Get it out, Mom! It's not a baby, it's an elephant! I can't do this!"

"Yes, you can," Maggie said, trembling worse than her daughter. Wildly, she looked around the room. "Jake, boil some newspapers and get the water I keep under the television!"

"What?"

"Hurry!" she shouted. "There's no time to argue. Oh, my God, it's crowning."

Dizzy, she caught on to the chair beside the table.

April screamed a scream that would have wakened someone who'd been dead for twenty years, and Jake got to his knees and pushed Maggie away.

"What are you doing?" she asked.

"I'm taking over," he said. "If anyone in this house is gonna deliver a baby, it's gonna be me."

Chapter Eight

"You can't deliver the baby!" Maggie screamed. "You know less about having babies than I do! At least I've *had* one!"

Jake spread a towel out beneath April's legs and began reaching for things in the kitchen drawers. "I've done this before, Maggie. Twins in a ski lodge at Lake Tahoe."

Maggie tried to steady her trembling, but she found that she was in worse shape than her daughter. "Twins? You delivered twins?"

"Yes. It was an emergency, just like this one."

April screamed and Maggie fell to her knees and began working off her daughter's underclothes. Panicked, she looked dubiously at Jake and decided that the story was too farfetched for him to have made up. "All right," she said. "The ambulance'll be here any minute, but if you've really done this before, just tell me what to do."

"I'll need some things," he said, laying a towel over April, despite her screaming and thrashing.

"Honey, it'll be all right!" Maggie shouted above April's pain. "Oh, Jake, what are we gonna do?"

"Just get me these things," he said. "And hurry. I'll need a lamp, preferably a gooseneck, a pair of scissors, some more towels, some string, some hydrogen peroxide and a Bud Light."

Without questioning him, Maggie scurried out of the room.

Her contraction ended, April lay there trying to catch her breath. "What are you going to do with all those things?" she whispered.

"I'm not sure," he said, glancing in the direction Maggie had gone. "Mostly they're just to distract your mother so you can stay calm. But, damn, I hope she hurries with that Bud Light."

Another contraction hit and April tightened up and let out another scream. "Calm down," Jake ordered in a voice that brooked no debate. "Breathe! Take a deep breath, then blow. Like this."

"No!" April screamed in a voice that suggested satanic possession. "That's not how they said to do it!"

"Then do it how they said to do it, damn it!" Jake yelled. "I don't know. I've never done this before!"

"You said you had!" she shouted, her tone rivaling Linda Blair's in *The Exorcist*. "You told my mother—"

She stopped short and let out another scream, and Jake saw the baby crowning. His first thought was to get up and run like hell, but he shunned it. His second was to stay and help the tiny life trying to get into the world, if for no other reason than to shut up April's screams.

Maggie rushed back into the room, her arms full of the items he had asked for. Instead of running to him, she ran to the refrigerator.

"Where are you going?" he shouted.

"To get the Bud Light! I got everything else."

"Forget the beer!" he shouted. "Bring me the disinfectant. The baby's coming."

"Oh, no!" She tossed him the disinfectant and dropped the other items onto the floor beside him.

She took one look at the baby's head crowning further and let out a loud moan. "Oh, my God. I'm calling the ambulance again."

Jake opened the bottle and poured the disinfectant over April's pelvis, and she let out another scream. In the living room, Jake heard Maggie yelling into the phone. When she slammed it down and came back into the kitchen, she said, "There's been a wreck on Sycamore and it's holding up traffic. The ambulance is stuck."

"Stuck!" Jake cried, his voice cracking. "You mean I'm really gonna have to do this?"

April shrieked again, and Jake cried, "Maggie, bring me that beer!"

As if he were a doctor asking for a scalpel, Maggie dashed to the refrigerator for the beer.

Jake popped the top and poured it down his throat, set the can down and looked at the job he had to face.

"Okay, everybody, stay calm. Maggie, boil some water and sterilize the string."

Grabbing the roll of string, Maggie obeyed. "What's this for?"

"The umbilical cord," he said. "This is how they did it on that 911 show on TV."

"Is this what you did with the twins?"

Distracted by the head crowning, Jake muttered, "What twins?"

Maggie swung around. "In Lake Tahoe."

"Oh, them. Yeah, I used it."

Maggie shot him a suspicious look, but he missed it. "Okay, April, we're almost there. I think one good push and this baby'll be here. Take a deep breath and push."

April caught her breath and pushed with all her might, and as more of the baby's head appeared, Maggie stumbled and caught the chair again. She was dizzy, he thought, and the water was boiling over. This moment from hell was his to deal with alone.

But as more and more of the baby's head pushed through, Jake realized that it wasn't so bad. Actually, it was kind of fascinating. His heart began to pound faster as the head began to emerge from the birth canal, and in a moment he saw the baby's swollen eyes, its little nose, its mouth.

In the most poignant burst of emotion he'd ever experienced in his life, he took hold of the little miracle, all slimy and warm and wet, and guided one shoulder out, then the other.

In seconds, the rest of the body was free, and for a moment there was silence as April experienced the profound relief of no more pain and Maggie gaped, speechless, at the miracle in Jake's hands.

He looked down at the little bundle of life, and in a voice that was shredded with emotion said, "It's a boy."

"A boy? Oh, Jake..." Maggie's tears took hold of her and she stood over him and the baby, savoring the sight of the little life.

"Give him to me," April whispered after a moment. "I want to hold my baby."

Jake handed her the child, and as she took it, she was overcome with her own tears. Jake rubbed his own eyes roughly, leaving them red.

A siren outside sounded, and within seconds paramedics were bursting into the kitchen, taking the baby and pulling April onto a gurney, taking the control and glory out of Jake's hands. He tried to fight the letdown feeling of being pushed out of the way as organized chaos quickly surrounded them.

When they began to roll April away on the gurney, Maggie kissed her and said, "Sweetheart, we'll be right behind you."

"Call Steve," April said weakly. "Tell him he has a son. He'll be sick he missed it."

"He'll get over it," Maggie said. "It couldn't be helped."

She and Jake followed the paramedics out and watched as they loaded mother and son into the ambulance. When it drove away, sirens still blaring, Maggie turned back to Jake. "You were wonderful," she whispered, sliding her arms around him.

His eyes filled with emotion, and he swallowed. "That was the most incredible experience of my life," he whispered. "I've never seen or felt anything like that before."

"What about the twins?" she asked.

"What twins?"

"Why do you keep asking me that?" she asked. "The ones you delivered at Lake Tahoe."

"Oh, those. Well, I wasn't exactly honest with you about that. They weren't exactly twins...actually, there were five of them. And they weren't babies, but dachshund puppies. And I didn't really deliver them. I just watched."

Her expression collapsed. "You lied to me!"

"Well, it wasn't a *malicious* lie," he mocked. "Just a little white lie. What else could I do? Let you pass out on top of April? I did what I had to do. Besides, I didn't lie about seeing it on TV."

Maggie burst into tears and threw her arms around his neck. "Oh, Jake, I'm so glad you were here. I would have botched things up so bad! There's no telling what I would have done."

"You'd have botched it up, all right," he admitted. "But I wouldn't have missed it for all the money in Palm Springs. Now let's go to the hospital. I want to get another look at your grandson."

"My grandson." She sighed on the word and looked, spacy eyed, in the direction of the ambulance. "Oh, Lord, I'm a grandmother."

Jake didn't comment on that observation. Instead, he handed her the phone to call Steve. When she had done her part in getting Steve riled up and frenzied, Jake took her hand and pulled her out to the Harley.

STEVE WAS ALREADY AT the hospital when they arrived, wringing his hands and mussing his hair, as if the ritual could restore some order to the chaos that had occurred without him. When he saw his mother-in-law, he turned on her, red faced. "Maggie, how could you let her have that baby without me?"

"Steve, we didn't have much choice. The baby was ready to come whether we wanted it to or not."

"But April was fine when I left. She wasn't even in labor. It was supposed to take hours, and I was supposed to have had plenty of time to get here."

Jake laughed and put his arm over the boy's shoulders. "Chill out, pal. The doctors didn't even make it in time."

Steve looked up at Jake, his face suddenly stricken. "They said you delivered it. I really appreciate it, man. Is it really a boy?"

"As far as I could tell." Jake laughed. "It's hard to make mistakes with things like that."

"Where's April?" Maggie asked. "Is she all right?"

"I don't know," Steve said. "It's all kind of confusing. I just got here myself, and the nurse was trying to find out something—"

At that moment the doors to the emergency room opened and a doctor burst out, pulling his mask down around his neck. He introduced himself to Steve, and said, "You can go be with your wife if you want. She's a little weak, but she's doing fine. We need to keep the baby in an incubator for a while. He's at least three weeks early, and we're running a few tests to make sure he doesn't have any lung problems."

"When can I see him?" Steve asked.

The doctor checked his watch. "Soon. Just go stay with April. As soon as the neonatologist gets through with him, we'll let you know. Trust us, Steve. Your son is in good hands, and he seems strong and healthy."

Steve released a huge sigh of relief and waved back at Maggie and Jake over his shoulder. "See you guys," he said. "I'm going to see about my family."

Maggie smiled at the paternal pride in his voice, and after a moment, she allowed Jake to pull her toward the waiting room. "I want to see my daughter," she said. "I want to make sure she's all right. It was so hectic at home—"

"They'll let you see her soon," he said. "But it's really Steve's place to be with her now."

Jake glanced in the direction Steve had gone. "I hope the baby's all right. What was that they were saying about his lungs?"

"That he's a little premature. There might be some problems."

"It's my fault, isn't it?" Jake asked suddenly.

Maggie gave him an astonished look. "How could it be?"

"Because I forgot to suction his throat. It hit me halfway to the hospital that I was supposed to wipe the mucus away and suction him. I saw that on *Night Court*, when all those women had those babies."

"Didn't the paramedics do it when they got there?"

"I don't know. Did they?"

Maggie smiled, took his hand and pressed a kiss on his cheek. "Jake, if it needed doing, they would have done it."

"But maybe I should have done it immediately. Maybe waiting caused some problems."

"No," she said. "You were wonderful. I couldn't believe how you took charge. You were a real hero. My grandbaby is going to grow up hearing about the wonderful man who delivered him."

Jake's grin was disbelieving and doubtful, and it faded quickly as his eyes glazed over and he stared across the room.

Maggie sat back on the vinyl couch and watched him staring, and she wondered why he was so pensive, so quiet. Yes, delivering a baby would shake anybody up, but that insecure voice in the back of her mind, the one that annoyed her at the most inopportune times, told her that he was pulling away. It had been bad enough when he'd come in and seen that April was really her mystery daughter. That in itself might have been enough for him to run the other way, but now the baby was real. He was here. And there was no denying that Maggie was a bona fide grandmother.

Not that she wanted to deny it, she thought, for she couldn't wait to hold that little life in her arms and coo to him and kiss his little soft cheek and smell that special scent only babies wore. That was what grandmothers were supposed to feel, not fear that their relationships with their college boyfriends would end.

Quietly, she and Jake sat holding hands, as Oprah came on the television perched high in one corner of the waiting room. And when she announced that today's topic was Older Women, Younger Men, Maggie wondered how she would scale the wall to reach the TV to turn it off. When she realized it was impossible, she thought of throwing her shoe at it with hopes of discreetly shattering the screen. But it didn't seem like a good idea. Jake seemed quietly transfixed as the audience responded to what they had been asked to judge. The response was divided. Half the audience thought it was great and that the older women should go for it. The other half thought it was selfish and perverted and that the older women should be ashamed.

When April's doctor interrupted the show just as the audience considered the Oedipus element of such relationships, Maggie considered throwing her arms around him and kissing him.

"The baby's very healthy," he said. "His lungs seem to be fully developed, and there don't seem to be any problems at all from the prematurity. He's with his mother right now, but if you two would like to put on some sterile gowns and masks, you're welcome to go in."

Maggie thanked him, and when he was gone, she turned back to Jake. "You don't have to come if you don't want to."

"Are you kidding?" he asked. "I delivered that baby. I have to make sure he's all right."

"You know, not too long ago, you were looking for something to ram your fist through."

"I know," he said with a sigh. "But delivering the baby took too much out of me. I'll do it later."

"Then you're still mad?"

Jake gave her a weary look. "I don't know. I need to think about it for a while. Come on."

He took her hand and led Maggie to April's room. They donned the gowns and masks the nurse handed them, and went through the door. The room was quiet and dark when they stepped into it.

"We had to draw the blinds so he'd open his eyes," April said softly, cradling the baby in her arms. "Oh, Mom, isn't he beautiful?"

Maggie's eyes welled up with tears, and the second strongest burst of love she had ever felt in her life exploded through her. The first had been when April was born. "Can I hold my grandson?" she asked.

Smiling serenely—a state Jake found surprising after her demonic screams of a couple hours before—April handed the baby to her mother. Jake looked over Maggie's shoulder at the tiny form, wiggling gently and looking around the room, as if saying, "So this is what the outside looks like."

Maggie held him, talking to him gently, cooing softly, until he drifted off to sleep. She started to hand him back to April, but Jake whispered, "Do you mind if I . . . ?"

Maggie looked up at him and saw that he wanted to hold the child. She looked from April to Steve, and both smiled their approval. Gently, she put the baby into his arms.

For the second time that day, she saw his eyes well over, glistening with emotion, and he smiled down at the baby. "You sure know how to make an entrance, don't you, kiddo?"

The baby sighed, and Jake bent down and kissed his cheek. Resting him in the crook of his elbow, he stroked back his soft hair with his other hand.

For the first time, it occurred to Maggie that Jake would make a wonderful father. But that fact saddened her, for she had never been more aware than at that moment that it could never happen with her. She was beyond childbearing...if not physically, then emotionally. She had spent the last eighteen years raising her child, and now she wanted to do as her daughter had suggested so often in the past few years, "get a life."

But Jake was not beyond it. He was at the prime age to begin parenthood, and there was some nice young woman out there who could give that to him. But it wasn't she.

Her eyes filled with tears again, not for the baby this time, but for the loss of hope that had suddenly confronted her. Maggie watched Jake hand the baby back to April, and heard him whisper, "He's beautiful, April. Really beautiful."

Then he turned away, wiped his eyes self-consciously and started for the door.

"Jake?"

It was April's quiet voice that stopped him, and he turned around. "I really appreciate all you did for me today," she said. "I hate to think what we would have done without you."

"It was nothing."

"Hardly nothing," she said, smiling down at her little son. "You were great. And we've decided to name him Andrew Jacob. Jacob is your real name, isn't it?"

Jake gaped at them, his face filling with emotion again. "You don't have to do that."

"Of course, we don't," April said. "But little Andy didn't have any ordinary birth. We wanted to do something to help him remember it."

"Wow." Jake smiled and looked at Maggie, and Maggie whispered, "We'll leave you two alone and come back in a little while. I have about two hundred phone calls to make."

But it wasn't the phone calls that occupied her mind now, but the emotion in Jake's face, his sudden quiet mood and the realizations she'd come to over the last hour. And as she set about the business of being a grandmother, she tried not to think about what it might mean to her and the man she had fallen in love with.

Maggie stayed at the hospital for a few more hours and saw the baby twice more, with Jake waiting patiently to take her home. He was quiet as they rode home, and when they got to her house, he told her he was beat and that he'd see her tomorrow.

Maggie watched from the front window of her living room as his motorcycle wound out of sight, and she wondered if he was, indeed, going home, or if he had gone out looking for some nice young woman who could distract him from the grandmother he'd gotten himself involved with. Someone with a fertile womb and a desire to bear his children,. Someone who hadn't lied to him about the major aspects of her own life.

Maggie went to the mirror in her bedroom, stared at her reflection and discovered that the witch was back. There was no getting rid of her for good. She would always be there, lurking under the surface of Maggie's makeup, reminding her who she really was and how foolish she was to think she was kidding anyone. Maggie breathed a sigh of defeat, and told herself it was as futile fighting her age as it was fighting her inevitable heartbreak. It was all just a matter if time.

JAKE SAT ON THE BACK DECK of his house, looking at the ocean as waves lapped against the shore in gentle rebellion against the breeze sweeping a chill through the air. He brought his gin and tonic to his lips and waited for it to soothe the turmoil in his soul. But it didn't help.

It had been a long day, and one that he would never forget as long as he lived. There was a new life in the world that hadn't been here yesterday, and he had helped get it here. The experience had moved him so profoundly that he hadn't had time to process it yet.

Could that be why he was sitting out here alone, getting drunk?

He tried to think it through, back to when he'd first felt the melancholy settling over him. It had been after the euphoria of delivering Andy had settled, after he'd had time to sit still and quiet. After he'd watched *The Oprah Winfrey Show*.

A May–December romance they called it, but he just called it love. And love didn't have age limits.

But it did for Maggie, he supposed, and that was why she'd lied to him about April. She had truly believed that his feelings would change if he knew she was going to be a grandmother.

And that fact told him a lot about how shallow she believed his feelings to be.

He bottomed the gin and tonic and let the anger rise like a tide in his soul. What else had she lied about? Was there a husband or two or three lurking in the bedrooms? Was there a prison record? A past life under an alias?

And what was he to her if she could see things as so temporary that she felt no need to come clean with him on a subject as obvious as the number of people living in her house?

She was going to dump him, and it occurred to him that he'd never been dumped before. It also occurred to him that he wouldn't like it—not one bit.

He got up and went back into the dark, lonely house and refilled his glass. Taking a deep, fortifying drink, he decided he had two choices.

He could let it happen, or he could fight like hell. And fighting came in a lot of forms. Tomorrow he'd show her just how hard he was to scare away.

Chapter Nine

It was barely past dawn when Maggie's doorbell rang three times consecutively, followed by an insistent, angry knock. Tying her robe around her nightgown, Maggie ran to answer it.

Looking out through the peephole, she saw Jake still ringing and knocking and looking as though he'd bang the door down if she didn't open it. Forgetting how awful she must look, she threw the door open.

Jake burst in and, taking her shoulders, kissed her before she could utter a word. His hands moved down her silk robe to contour the shape of her buttocks, and she felt his arousal through his jeans, the incessant hammering of his heart, the warmth of his breath whispering through her.

He broke the kiss, and she caught her breath, but suddenly he had gathered her gown up to her hips and his hand moved across bare flesh over her stomach, her ribs, her breasts....

He pushed her robe off her shoulders and worked the strap of her nightgown down her arm until her breast was exposed. Taking it in his mouth, he lifted her into his arms and carried her to her bedroom.

Just inside the door, Maggie reached for the light switch and flicked it off.

Jake set her down beside the bed, still not speaking a word, and slipped the other strap off. The gown slipped down her hips and puddled at her feet.

Before she knew what had happened, he had torn off his own clothes and had thrown her down on the bed. He was so forceful and demanding that she found herself more aroused than she'd ever been before— aroused to the extent that she gasped for breath and her heart pounded a lethal rhythm and her skin glistened with a sheen produced only by unutterable ardor.

Their union was dangerous in its excitement, rushed in its fervor, frenzied in its desperation. Jake's passion fluctuated from control to madness, while hers rotated between craziness and starvation. Together, they climbed the crest of their excitement, held there in sweet agony for a long moment, then burst into a thousand fragmented pieces that only the other had the power to reassemble.

Afterward, they lay in a sleepy, tangled embrace, and Maggie realized that as yet, neither had spoken a word today.

"Jake?" she asked, hating to break the spell of physical communication that seemed so much greater than mere words could achieve. "What brought that on?"

She felt him smiling against her mouth. "This morning I woke up and realized I didn't kiss you last night," he said, tickling her lips with the rumble of his voice. "And I just wasn't willing to start today without taking care of that unfinished business."

She wondered if he could see the enchantment glistening in her eyes. "You were kind of in a daze last night. You had me a little worried."

"Yeah," he whispered. "So were you. But we both seem clearer headed now."

He pulled her into another long, lingering kiss, one that stirred her senses to life and made her forget all the reasons she wasn't right for him. Clearheadedness did wonders for denial, she thought. And it opened a certain path for those raging emotions she couldn't escape. When the kiss broke, Jake kept his lips against hers and whispered, "I love making love to you, Maggie."

"You do?" she whispered weakly.

"I do," he said. "You drive me crazy."

She swallowed and looked up at him. "Me, too."

"You know, we wasted last night. April and Steve weren't home and you could have stayed with me."

"You seemed to want to be alone. You were still pretty mad at me."

"Maybe just a little. But would you have? If I'd suggested it?"

"I don't know."

"What if I suggest it tonight?" he whispered.

Maggie pulled back enough to look at him. "I don't know. Let's just wait and see."

"I want to sleep with you, Maggie. In a bed, with my eyes closed and my arms around you. I want to wake up with you."

He kissed her again, once more arousing emotions she had spent the entire night telling herself she didn't need. Suddenly she wasn't quite as convinced that setting him free would be the right thing. He smelled too good, and his arms were too powerful and safe. Despite the truths he knew about her now, he still seemed crazy about her, even after making love to her—albeit in the dark—and experiencing her grandmotherhood firsthand.

It was a miracle, that was all. Just like the birth of little Andy in her kitchen.

So she decided that she'd abide by one of her long-standing rules about making decisions when she was under stress. She wouldn't make any decisions at all.

"Will you, Maggie?" he whispered against her hair. "Will you sleep in my bed with me tonight?"

"I think so," she whispered, but even as she spoke, she couldn't help wondering at the wisdom of this whole affair in which there could really be no winners and heartbreak lurked just around the corner. She didn't know how long she could hold it back, she thought, but it was gaining fast. And she knew it was just a matter of time.

"WE'VE MADE A DECISION," April announced later that morning when Maggie came in to see her and the baby in the hospital. Steve sat in the corner of the room, rocking his son and humming a lullaby. It was a sweet sight, one Maggie wouldn't have anticipated from a man who wore one earring and had a tattoo of Popeye on his arm. The sight made her feel that, just maybe, Steve wouldn't be a failure at everything.

"What decision?" she asked, keeping her voice low.

"About staying home with the baby," April said. "We already knew I would do it, but now we've figured out how Steve can do it, too."

Maggie tried to keep her face calm, but she couldn't help the reaction crying out in her brain. *Don't tell me, let me guess. The plan is for me to get two more jobs,*

*quit school and spend the rest of my life supporting
your family.* Instead, she said, "April, don't you think
it's unrealistic for both of you to stay home? Have you
forgotten that little matter of paying bills? Buying
food?"

"Just listen," Steve cut in, coming to his feet and
handing the baby to Maggie, as if that would keep her
from blowing her top. "We've got this all figured out.
We just need a little help from you."

No kidding, she wanted to say, but instead she gritted her teeth and said, "What kind of help?"

"We're going to open a nursery!" April said trium-
phantly, her eyes dancing as she waited for Maggie to
jump for joy, too.

Maggie disappointed her. "A nursery?"

"Yes," Steve said. "We're going to start keeping
children at home."

"Home?" Maggie asked cautiously. "Whose
home?"

"Well, *our* home, of course," April said. "Where
else?"

Maggie shook her head, but fought hard not to raise
her voice with the sleeping child in her arms. "Wait a
minute. That is *my* home, April. Don't you think you
should consult a person first before you turn her home
into a business?"

"We *are* consulting you," Steve said, cutting in
again. "Right now, we're consulting."

Maggie rolled her eyes and decided to sit down.
"Just how many kids do you propose to keep?"

"Ten or twelve," Steve said. "That way, we could
make a pretty nice living and we could still stay home
with Andy. Tell her the best part, April."

April beamed. "We're going to call it . . . Grandma's House."

Maggie's face blanched to the color of stone. "Grandma's House," she repeated, trying not to let her voice tremble. "You're going to put a sign out in front of my house, that says Grandma's House?"

"Yes! It's a great promotional gimmick," Steve said. "People will picture home and safety and love, and they'll bring their little ones to us. It'll be great. And don't worry, Maggie, because you won't even know they're there."

She wondered if blood pressure had ever blown off the top of anyone's head. "You think I won't notice twelve kids running all over my house?" she asked through her teeth.

"No," he said, "because they won't get there until you're gone to school in the mornings, and by the time you get home from work in the afternoons, their parents will have picked them up. Meanwhile, we'll have an income, and we won't have to keep borrowing from you. . . ."

She had to admit that that part sounded appealing. But not appealing enough. "Steve, it's my home. I don't like opening it up to a bunch of strangers."

"They won't be strangers long," he said. "Besides, we'll keep them busy and they won't hurt anything. How hard could it be, after all? You play a couple of games in the mornings, change a few diapers, feed them something for lunch, then make them take a nap. By then, their parents will come. Piece of cake."

Afraid of what harm she'd do the baby, holding him while her blood pressure reached such volatile levels, Maggie handed Andy back to April. Forcing herself to remain calm, she turned back to her son-in-law.

"Steve, *one* child is not a piece of cake. A dozen kids is pure hell. Hasn't anyone ever told you that the work kids create is increased exponentially?"

"What's that?" Steve asked.

She rolled her eyes again. "It means that three kids are not three times more trouble than one, they're *nine* times more trouble. That means twelve kids are a hundred and forty-four times more trouble! That means people losing their minds, property being destroyed—"

"Maggie, is it your PMS time again? You seem to be blowing this all out of proportion."

"No, it's not my PMS time, Steve!" Maggie whispered dramatically.

"Menopause, then?"

If it could have happened, her head would have shot off at that moment. That it remained attached was encouraging to her. "I'm not old enough for menopause!" she said with a hiss. "But insanity isn't out of the question, especially used as a plea at my murder trial!"

Steve grinned and shot his wife an I-told-you-she-was-crazy look. "Chill out, Maggie. You're getting all worked up."

"Worked up? Steve, it's just occurred to me that my life and my home are never going to be the same. And it isn't even little Andy's fault!"

April got Oscar-caliber tears in her eyes. "Mom, how can you say that? This could solve all of Steve's career problems. He'll have a management position at the nursery. Heck, he'll *own* it, and Andy will get the best possible care from both of us."

"April, honey, it isn't that easy. You have no idea—"

"Are you saying that your daughter is going to be a bad mother?" Steve interjected.

"No, of course not!"

"Then why couldn't she take care of a few more? We both love kids."

Maggie leaned her head back against her chair and closed her eyes, trying desperately to fight the headache entrenching itself behind her eyes. This conversation was asinine. The very idea was ludicrous. And it wasn't even worth an argument. The venture would last about fifteen minutes, and then Steve would move on to some other cockamamy idea. The sooner she gave in, the sooner it would be over.

She opened her eyes and glared at April and Steve, both sitting on the bed like children playing with a doll. "All right," she said on a sigh. "I guess we can try it, just to see how it works out. But no sign. I will not advertise that this is Grandma's House."

Simultaneously, they protested. "If we don't have a sign, no one will know about us," Steve said. "If we have to rely on newspaper ads and stuff, we'll have to have money. If we could just put one simple little sign out front, with a grand opening banner stuck across it, it wouldn't cost much and it would serve all the purpose we need it to."

Maggie groaned. "I can't believe this!"

"Mom, please. You won't even know it's there. Besides, it's true. It *is* Grandma's house."

Steve and April shared a chuckle, but Maggie didn't crack a smile. For a moment she considered hurling a vase across the room and hitting her son-in-law right between the eyes—not to kill him, but just to debilitate him enough so that he'd quit coming up with these harebrained schemes that kept messing up her life. She wanted to run away as fast and far as she could, to someplace where she could be herself without constant reminders that she was over the hill.

She pulled up out of the chair, suddenly feeling very old, and started for the door. "Put the sign up," she said through her teeth. "Pave the front yard and put in a playground. Paint all the windows hot pink. Put zebra stripes on the siding. Do whatever you want."

April beamed again. "Thanks, Mom. You won't regret it."

Not believing how dense her daughter and son-in-law were, Maggie pushed out of the door.

JAKE WAS STANDING AT the hospital nursery window when Maggie came out, gazing in at the babies lined up in their little beds. He turned to her with an amused grin on his face when she approached him. "I was just trying to pick out the ones who would be the next big shots of our country," he said. "See that one over there, screaming his lungs out? He's gonna be the next Mick Jagger, and the one over there with the pacifier will be the next Louis Armstrong. Oh, and the one over there with the birthmark— I've named her Gorbachev. And the one that keeps rooting against the head of her bed . . . that's Margaret Thatcher."

"Sounds like you've got the whole nursery pegged. Which one's going to be president?"

"The president's out," he said. "He's with April and Steve."

Maggie grinned. "You think Andy's going to be president?"

"Well, how could he be anything less? I delivered him, didn't I?"

She smiled as his eyes drifted back over the cribs, but as she realized the joy he seemed to glean from the babies, her smile faded. And then she remembered Grandma's House and the dozen kids usurping her home and her oblivious daughter and son-in-law taking over her life.

Jake looked down at her, and he instantly lost his own smile. "What's the matter, darlin'?"

Tears sprang to her eyes, and she shook her head. "Nothing. Just the kids. They've got some scheme to turn my house into a nursery so they can both stay at home."

Jake shrugged. "Just tell them no."

Maggie's look told him he didn't know what he was talking about. "And destroy any hope for their ever supporting themselves?"

"Maggie, they don't have to rely on you to help them do that."

"Either they rely on me to help them do it, or *I'll* be the one who supports them. I honestly don't think it would bother them a bit for me to quit school and go back to work full-time so I could feed them. But I'm not going to do it. It's my turn."

He put his arm around her shoulders and turned her away from the nursery. "Let's go home, kiddo," he said. "You need to get your mind off all this."

And as she let Jake lead her out of the hospital, Maggie realized that her problems couldn't be escaped. They were as binding and permanent as motherhood.

She only wished love could be that lasting.

THE SIGHT OF HER HOUSE invoked different emotions than ever before when Maggie pulled up to it in her car with Jake beside her. Tonight it represented her loss of control, the dismal future she had to look forward to and the fact that all her dreams were quickly being shot to hell.

But at the same time that those emotions reached her consciousness, she felt a twang of guilt that she should feel them at all. Wasn't a mother supposed to be self-sacrificing? Wasn't a grandmother supposed to be generous?

"You okay?" Jake's voice cut into her reverie, and Maggie looked at him, then back at her house.

"Yeah, fine."

"Well . . . are we gonna get out or just sit here?"

Maggie didn't move. "I was just trying to picture it. My house filled with a dozen screaming kids. Everything broken and sticky. And April and Steve liking it here so much that they never want to leave."

"It's your life, Maggie," Jake said. "If you don't like it, change it."

Her sigh carried the weight of her burden. "I can't."

"Yes, you can."

Unable to argue the point further, she got out of the car and headed inside. Idly, she tossed her purse onto the couch and scuffed into the kitchen to pour them each a drink. Jake followed her.

He leaned against the counter and watched her fill their glasses with ice. "I'm serious, Maggie. You don't have to let them run all over you."

"So what am I supposed to do?" she asked. "Throw them out into the street? Steve doesn't even have a job, and that little baby is my grandson."

"Well, you could put your foot down about the nursery."

"And support them? I can't handle that much longer without quitting school."

"Charge them rent. *Make* Steve work."

"I can't make Steve do anything. Besides, I don't want my daughter and grandson living in poverty. Personally, I wouldn't be torn up if Steve starved to death, but April and Andy... I've at least got to give them a chance to help themselves." Maggie handed Jake his glass, then waved the subject off. "Really, I'd rather not talk about it anymore."

Jake set down his glass and pulled her to him. "Come here," he whispered.

She went willingly, but her heart felt heavier than she remembered it being in years. She looked into his eyes, saw the peace and comfort there, the safety and protectiveness, and wondered how he could offer her that when he was ten years her junior.

And yet as Jake pulled her into a deep hug that didn't end for several minutes, Maggie realized that she had never felt so protected before. For the first time in her life, she seemed to have someone in her corner.

But it was all wrong.

Jake was still a young man, one who had a chance for a future and a family, one who needed someone his own age to grow old with him. Not someone with such a head start on him. He needed someone who would make love to him with the lights on, who wouldn't get tired so much earlier, who didn't have built-in family problems waiting to tackle her.

Quietly she pulled out of his embrace, and whispered, "We need to talk."

Apprehension colored his eyes, and he asked, "What about?"

"About us," she said.

She went across the kitchen, putting two yards between them, and leaned back on the counter facing him. His eyes were wary and guarded as he watched her.

"Jake, I don't think we should see each other anymore."

For a moment he only looked at her, silent, and the thought flitted through her mind that it might have been exactly what he wanted her to say. Terror filled her heart, terror that he wouldn't fight her, that he'd take her word and leave.

Terror that he wouldn't.

His voice was gently controlled when he answered. "Is there any particular reason you've come to this insane conclusion?"

"Lots of them," she said, fighting the tears wrestling with her eyes.

"Let me guess," he said. "Your age, right?"

"That's part of it," she said. "But the age thing is only a symbol of so many other things."

"Care to share them with me?"

Maggie sighed and wondered how she could say things that he'd never understand, things that sounded presumptuous, as if she expected them to be heading for marriage. That was ridiculous; she knew he would never consider marrying a grandmother. But that, in itself, was part of the problem, she supposed.

"Maggie, I'm waiting," he said. "You may think you can get rid of me with one little announcement that we're over, but I'm a little tougher to scare away than that."

She wanted to smile, but there wasn't one left in her heart. "Jake, I feel like I'm starting to make an emotional investment here. And I can't possibly get a return on it. The payoff is impossible, and—"

"Are we talking about mutual funds or us?" he said coldly.

She sighed and rubbed her temples where a headache was starting to form. She told herself that beating around the bush wasn't fair to either of them, for it left too much to misinterpretation. She had to be straightforward. She had to shoot from the hip.

"Jake, I know myself too well. When I get involved with someone, like I've done with you, I can fall pretty hard. I start wanting things. If I start to love someone, I start thinking in terms of commitment, permanency...."

She hesitated, waiting for him to balk, but he didn't.

"So what's the problem?" he asked softly.

"We can't think in those terms about each other," she said. "It would be crazy. I'm so much older than you, and I have a bushel of problems, and our just being attached to each other the way we've been isn't good for you. As long as I'm around, you won't meet the right person when she comes along."

"The right person?" he asked, amusement lacing his eyes. "And what on earth makes you so sure it's not you?"

Maggie smiled a gentle smile, but her heart was breaking. "Oh, Jake. It can't be me. I saw you with little Andy yesterday. You were wonderful. And today in front of the nursery... You'd be a terrific father, but I'm forty years old and still struggling to get my own child raised. I don't want to have any more children!"

"Maggie, what on earth makes you think I want to be a father?"

"Well, why wouldn't you? Anybody who could look like that when he holds a baby—"

"Not just any baby, Maggie. The baby I delivered. I've never witnessed a birth before, let alone delivered a baby myself. How could I hold that baby and not get emotional?"

"But it must have awakened your dreams of being a father, Jake. You don't have to hide it from me. The whole conversation is ridiculous because it isn't like we were talking about marriage, anyway, and we certainly don't have a commitment between us. But if there can't be one—and there can't—then I don't want to get more involved with you. It's just too hard."

Jake stared at her, silent, for a long moment, and in those seconds, Maggie convinced herself that he was weighing the wisdom of her words and deciding that she was right. Which she knew she was. But something deep inside her wanted him to convince her otherwise.

"Maggie, I have a lot of dreams," he said finally, in a voice rough and husky and emotion packed. "But being a father has never been one of them. I'm not looking for a baby factory. If I've been looking at all, it was for someone I could love, someone who could make my heart do funny things every time she walks into a room. Someone I can't stand to go a day without seeing."

"But, Jake, that kind of chemistry is so temporary. Family's the only thing that lasts. I can't believe it isn't important to you, and I can't go on with you knowing I can't give it to you."

Jake closed his eyes, struggling with the emotion taking over his face, and when he opened them, they were glistening with feeling. "Maggie, why does it have to be so serious? Why can't we just keep seeing each other, see how it goes?"

"Because it hurts too much. I'll get more and more attached to you. If there's no future, what's the point?"

"How can there *be* a future if you don't give it a chance?"

"Because I don't *want* there to be a future with you!" she shouted. "Because I don't want to constantly be looking over my shoulder for someone in a bikini to come along and distract you from me. I don't want to constantly feel inadequate and ugly and old next to you, and I don't want to feel that I'm holding you back from anything you have the potential to be. I'm a grandmother, Jake, and if you ever wound up marrying me, you'd be a grandfather! A thirty-year-old grandfather! Chew on that for a while and see how you like it!"

Jake sat staring at her, his eyes still filled with pain, and when he spoke, his voice was shaky. "Maggie, I don't want to stop seeing you."

Her voice trembled as he spoke. "It's the best thing, Jake," she said. "And the sooner we get it over with, the better."

They stared at each other for what seemed an eternity, until finally, Jake whispered, "So that's it? Just like that?"

"There's no easy way," she managed to say.

His eyes glistened as he whispered, "Do I at least get a kiss goodbye?"

Timidly, not knowing if it was wisdom or foolishness that sent her into his arms, she went. Jake crushed her against him, holding her in a shattering embrace, and when he kissed her, his kiss was full of despair and desperation, agony and pleading, and something that she was almost sure was love.

But love was the worst reason to have a relationship, she'd always been told. It was the worst reason to let one continue. It was the worst reason to hold someone back.

But it was the best reason to set someone free.

Maggie broke the kiss, stepped away from him and looked down at the floor, unable to meet his eyes.

Finally, when he realized there was nothing left to say, Jake took his helmet off the counter, turned back for one last look and saying nothing else, walked out of her life.

Chapter Ten

Jake rode his Harley faster and harder than he'd ever ridden it, until he reached some town he couldn't name and came close to running out of gas. Then filling the tank again, he turned around and headed back home, determined to ride Maggie out of his system once and for all.

The irony of it all filled him to the brim, making him angry and agonized at the same time, making him want to scream and laugh and cry—feelings he had rarely felt for a woman before. Usually there was no emotion, no feeling at all. Just satisfied pleasures. Just satiated lust.

But this was different. For the first time in his life, he'd found someone who could make him feel more. Someone who could make him think about her—and her alone—every hour of the day. Someone who occupied his heart as much as his mind.

And she had dumped him.

He tore off his helmet and strapped it between his legs, and let the wind blow through his hair, warning him of the hazard of the speed he was climbing toward. But he didn't slow down until he reached his house.

He thought of pulling into his driveway, giving up the fight, but the wind was strong and the waves whipped loudly against the shore, thrashing like angry horses in a wild pasture. Pulling his bike onto the sand, he rode down to the edge of the water and rode as fast as his bike would take him, sending a spray of water up and over him until he was soaked and exhausted.

And still he didn't feel better.

It was nearly midnight when he reached his house and walked into the dark loneliness that had never bothered him before, in fact it had once been his dearest friend. Now he hated it as if it had betrayed him.

He left the lights off and lay in the dark, still in his wet clothes, staring at the ceiling, rehashing Maggie's words today as if he could make more sense of them now. She had dumped him because she had thought he wanted to be a father. She had dumped him because of her age. She had dumped him because she was a grandmother.

But didn't she realize that the idea of being a grandfather was more appealing to him than fatherhood? He grinned at the thought of being a thirty-year-old grandfather—and at the thought of little Andy growing up with Steve for a father. That kid would need a good grandfather figure to guide him. Someone to play with him, teach him to make sand sculptures, school him in Frisbee throwing, then give him back to his parents when he got tired and ornery. He would need someone like Jake to keep him in line.

As if a light had been turned on in his dark house, Jake sat up straight and caught his breath. It was easy, he thought. All he had to do was convince Maggie that she couldn't get rid of him. All he had to do was show her that he didn't want children of his own and that her own phobias were silly. All he had to do was something no one had ever really done for her before.

All he had to do was love her.

He grabbed his helmet and still not bothering to change clothes, rushed back to his bike and cranked it up.

He was going to Maggie's, he told himself, and he would stop at nothing before getting her to take him back.

THE TELEVISION FLASHED silently in the corner of Maggie's living room, in what she thought would probably be the last quiet night she would spend here. Tomorrow April and Steve would bring Andy home and nothing would ever be the same again. She looked forward to it, as she had told them when she'd gone to see them this afternoon after Jake left. But there was a small part of her that mourned the life she had expected to forge out for herself now.

And a big part of her mourned the loss of Jake.

Already she felt his absence in every fiber of her body—the absence of his arms around her, the absence of his windy scent, the absence of his warmth, the absence of the sizzling chemistry he had left smoldering within her. The telephone sat mutely, waiting for her to pick it up and call him, but she had been through heartache before. She knew better than to go back on a decision she had made logically and rightly. She knew better than to undo the process of forgetting him just to soothe the ache in her heart.

The doorbell rang, and, frowning, she pulled herself off the couch and went to look through the peephole. She saw Jake standing in the circle of light on the porch, and for a moment she hesitated.

"Open the door, Maggie," he said. "I know you're there."

Sighing, she pulled open the door. He pushed through and closed it behind him.

"Jake, I told you—"

"I don't care what you told me." He took her shoulders in his hands and stared down at her with eyes full of fire and fight. "I don't care what you think or what noble gesture you think you're making. I didn't come back here for you. I came back here for me."

"But it's wrong, Jake." Her voice broke. "One or both of us is bound to get hurt."

"I'm hurting now, Maggie," he whispered, sliding his arms around her and pressing his forehead against hers. "And so are you, or you wouldn't have those tears in your eyes."

"Jake, please..."

"Maggie, I don't know all the reasons why I've got you so deep under my skin, but I know that I've had plenty of other chances to feel this way, and I just never have before. You're the only woman who's ever been able to bring me to my knees and, damn it, I have no intention of letting you go!"

"But, Jake, look at me! What do you see? A forty-year-old grandmother!"

"When I look at you, Maggie, I see a beautiful, fascinating, intelligent, sexy woman who makes my blood heat up every time I think of her. When I look at you, Maggie, I see perfection. I see hope."

"Perfection? Oh, Jake, that just shows you how unrealistic your image of me is. I'm not perfect. I look every minute of my age... and then some."

"So what do you think will happen if I discover that? If I find out you aren't perfect?"

"You'll probably run like hell," she said. "You'll probably wake up and ask yourself what in the world was wrong with you to fall for someone like me."

"You think so?" he asked, his lips hovering just above hers, teasing her with his closeness. "Then prove it. Make love to me in the light. Repulse me. Send me running. If you really want me to go and you're so sure I will, then make love to me in the light, Maggie."

Her heart flipped like the finely oiled blades of a fan with the power to destroy anything that got in its way. She felt that same heart liquefying in her chest, melting into her bloodstream, making it hotter as his lips fell to hers and his hands moved down to her hips.

And suddenly she forgot all the reasons why she wanted him out of her heart and her home.

He lifted her in his arms, his power and strength making her feel small and secure, and carried her through her house to her bed. He let her feet slide down his legs as he reached for the lamp. Reluctant, Maggie reached out and stopped him, but he pulled his hand away and turned on the light, bathing the room in soft golden hues.

"Jake..." she whispered, but he kissed her again, quieting her and quieting the fears nestling in her heart. His hands moved between them to her blouse and slowly, he began unbuttoning it.

"I'm scared," she whispered, but as if he didn't hear, he slid her blouse over her shoulders and dropped it to the floor. His hands moved to her bra, deftly unfastened it and peeled it away.

He kissed her with an urgency that warned her of what was to come. His hands dropped to the khakis she still wore, and slowly, he opened the zipper.

She tried to protest, but he slid them over her hips as the kiss deepened, then he abandoned her mouth and bent low to pull them off, one leg at a time. He knelt as she stepped out of them, and he slid his hands up her legs, his gaze scanning every inch of her. There wasn't repulsion in his eyes, she realized, but a smoky longing, a desperate need to have and feel and know her.

He slid his hands under the elastic legs of her panties and pulled them down, slowly removing the last remnant of her covering with deliberate, breath-held reverence.

When she was naked, he rose up, sliding his hands up her thighs and hips, feeling every flaw that she knew existed. But suddenly she wasn't ashamed, for his breath was as shallow as it had been in the dark, his eyes were as misty, his voice as hoarse, his arousal as apparent.

And suddenly she was tearing at his own clothes, unable to get them off fast enough, and they fell into bed, flesh against flesh, heart against heart, man against woman, uniting quickly and urgently, desperately seeking the permanence that each of them feared.

When their passion was spent and their hormones functioned at less than dangerous levels again, Jake raised up on his elbows and touched her face with a trembling hand. "I love you, Maggie. And I'm not going anywhere."

Her heart sang as she pulled him into her arms and held him until the sun intruded on their morning. But the light didn't frighten her now, for Jake had seen her the way she was.

And he was still here.

THE ALARM CLOCK WENT OFF at the usual time, and Maggie sat up and looked around, groggy. Jake was lying with his hands clasped behind his head, grinning at her.

"You're cute in the morning," he said.

Maggie covered her face and shoved her fingers through her hair. "Oh, no. I must look like a witch."

"An enchantress, maybe," he teased, raising up on an elbow and pulling her hands away from her face. She tried to turn away, but he grabbed her and wrestled her back down.

"Don't hide from me, Maggie," he said. "You're beautiful, and you know it."

"Jake, you can't be serious."

"I am," he whispered. "Now shut up and kiss me."

They made love again, long, sleepy love, until finally, it was time for Jake to get ready for class. As they ate a quick breakfast of bacon and toast, which Jake cooked as Maggie was showering, he put his arms around her again. "I'm going to miss you at school today."

"It can't be helped," she said. "April will need me when she brings the baby home. I don't even think she knows how to bathe a baby. I need to be here for Andy's homecoming."

"I'll take care of getting assignments for you," he said. "And I'll see you this afternoon?"

"Yeah," she said. "I'm taking off work today, too."

He pulled her against him and looked down at her, his arms making her feel small and young again. "Hey, about that Grandma's House thing? Don't sweat it, okay? Just try to enjoy your grandbaby without worrying about all that other stuff."

He kissed her forehead, then let go of her and started for the door. Before he was out of it, she said, "Jake?"

He turned back.

"Thanks for not running."

"You won't get rid of me that easy," he said with a wink, and then he was gone.

Maggie stared at the door for a moment after she'd heard him drive away, marveling at the fact that he had told her he loved her last night.

He loved her? The absurdity and wonder of that filled her with joy, and she closed her hand over her mouth and told herself it wasn't a dream. This morning he had seen her without makeup and he had liked what he'd seen.

What did it all mean?

The phone rang, interrupting her reverie, and she picked it up quickly.

"Hello?"

"Mom? Are you ready to come get us?"

Maggie smiled. "I sure am. Have you got everything ready?"

"Yes," April said, her voice quiet, and Maggie knew that she was probably holding Andy. "They said we'd be ready to check out in about half an hour."

"I'll be right there, honey. Give Andy a kiss for me, okay?"

"I will."

Maggie set the phone back in its cradle and ambled into the room April and Steve had been using. There wasn't space for a crib, so they'd probably have to put it in the living room. But it would all work out somehow, she thought. It would have to.

Thoughts of those dozen children running through her house sent her pulse reeling again, but taking Jake's advice, Maggie put it out of her mind. April and Steve had probably dismissed that idea already, she thought. They were probably already on to some new scheme of his. Something simple and unpretentious, like executive at IBM or brain surgery. One never knew with Steve.

Feeling happier and lighter than she had felt in days, Maggie left her house, realizing that it would never be that quiet again. But it was okay—last night had given her enough memories to last a lifetime. And no amount of chaos could override that.

Chapter Eleven

There was no denying that Andy had a good set of lungs. The moment April carried him into Maggie's house, he let out a scream that could have awoken the corpses at the cemetery ten miles away. And he didn't stop crying until the next morning, when it was time for Maggie to go to school.

Sometime during the melee the night before, Jake had come by with her assignments—assignments that she had not had the time to even read—and seeing the chaos, he had wisely slipped back out as quickly as he could. Maggie had fought the urge to go with him and had earnestly begun her grandmotherly tenure.

Now at 7:00 a.m., she stood in front of the mirror trying to cover the bags beneath her eyes and the re-defined lines on her face. Andy was determined to make her look like his grandmother, she thought, and before it was over, she was afraid he would succeed.

Desperate not to disturb the quiet, she tiptoed through the living room, where April lay on the couch sound asleep with her new baby nestled against her. Steve had sacked out on the floor, as if it would be a huge betrayal to actually sleep in the bed while his wife was losing her mind with his son. She had to hand it to

him, Maggie thought. Steve hadn't balked at the responsibility last night. He had been right there with
April every moment of the night.

And so had Maggie.

They had to work out a schedule, she told herself as
she gathered her books and slipped out the back door,
feeling as though she had been beaten and denied sleep
for three days. They needed to get it across to each
other that *someone* in the house had to sleep. If one
was up, the other two should be napping. Otherwise,
they would all snap at the same time and little Andy
would be on his own before his one-month birthday.

Which she wasn't so sure he couldn't handle, judg-
ing by the way he'd run the household last night.

Presidential material, she thought with a soft grin.
Maybe Jake was right.

She went outside and shivered at the bite in the air.
It was an unseasonably cool day, the kind that sent
Florida natives into a tailspin of digging out the win-
ter clothes they hadn't expected to need until January.
Maggie hadn't had time, however, so she had pulled a
jacket over her short-sleeved blouse. Shivering, she got
into her car and flicked on the heater as she cranked the
engine.

Basking in the quiet of her car, she drove to school,
fighting to stay awake. When she pulled into the parking lot in front of the Fine Arts Building, she saw Jake
leaning against the wall, waiting for her in a red cable
knit sweater and an open leather jacket, his hands ca-
sually hidden in the pockets. A smile came to her lips
despite her fatigue.

He approached her before she'd even gotten out of
her car, pressed a kiss on her lips and took her load of
books. "How's it goin', kiddo?"

"Don't ask."

"That bad, huh? Is Andy learning how to push his grandma's buttons?"

"He's pushing everybody's buttons. He's got his days and nights mixed up, and I don't know how we're going to set him straight. Meanwhile, I didn't do any homework, I haven't even opened the books, and I have that test tomorrow that I can't possibly pass...."

"Come to my house tonight," he said, as if that would solve everything. "Study over there."

"I can't." She hooked a hand through his arm as they headed across campus. "April might need help, and I'd just fall asleep anyway."

"Maggie, you have to sleep sometime. Are you working today?"

"Of course," she said wearily. "Somebody has to."

"Then let me help."

Maggie's eyebrows drew together in disbelief. "You've got to be kidding. You probably don't even know how to change a diaper."

"Hey, you're talking to the man who delivered that baby. You think I can't figure out how to change a diaper?"

She laughed. "Yeah, you probably could. But really, we've got it under control."

"*They've* got it under control...you're just *being* controlled."

Maggie kept walking, but he stopped her and grabbed her arm, making her face him. "Maggie, here's what we're gonna do, and I won't take no for an answer. You come to my house after work to study, and I'll go to your house and cook supper for the kids. And then I'll play with Andy for a while—a little football maybe, and we might brush up on our Frisbee throwing, and I'll read a story—and give April and Steve a chance to nap before I have to leave.''

Maggie gaped up at him, astonished. ''I can't let you do that.''

''Well you have no choice. It's a done deal.''

''But, Jake—''

''Hey, Maggie, you've invested a lot into coming back to school, and I'll be damned if I'm gonna stand back and watch while you let some little three-day-old devil take it away from you. That might be okay with April and Steve, but it's not okay with me. Now go to class. You're gonna be late.''

''But I can't—''

''Go,'' he said, kissing her again. ''I'll see you at The Grill for lunch. Go!''

And before she could protest further, he had sauntered off across the lawn to his own class.

JAKE DECIDED THAT NIGHT that hell was the sound of a screaming baby's voice, the smell of sour diapers overflowing in a diaper pail and Steve's inane ramblings about all the plans he had for the nursery he was opening in two weeks. Jake hoped Maggie was having a good night studying, because he didn't intend to do this many more times in his life.

He'd had to wash the plates before he'd set the table, since every plate in the house had been dirty—which he was quite sure hadn't been the way Maggie had left the house that morning. The pungent aroma of spaghetti filled the air, and he smiled because he'd done such a great job despite the chaos around him.

''And I was thinking of building a playground in the back yard,'' Steve was saying. ''I've been putting together this diagram of what it'll look like. Tunnels,

Tarzan vines, tire swings, and I plan on going around to garage sales Saturday to buy up all the riding toys I can get my hands on...that is, if I can get Maggie to loan me a little cash."

Jake feigned an interested look at the diagram and set the plates on the table. April came in, bouncing her screaming child up and down, and Jake smiled in amusement that the girl suddenly looked older than her mother. "I'm starved," she said. April looked at the spaghetti steaming on the table, and her face fell. "Oh, no. Spaghetti?"

Jake turned around, bracing himself. "What's wrong?"

"I can't eat spaghetti," she said. "Didn't Mom tell you?"

"All *Mom* told me was that you were nursing and I had to make you eat. She didn't tell me there was anything you couldn't eat."

"Well, that's why," she said. "*Because* I'm nursing. The tomato sauce will give Andy colic."

Jake looked dumbly at her. "How will we know the difference?"

"I don't know," she cried, "but I can't eat something that I *know* will give him colic. He'll never stop crying."

"He never stops crying, anyway."

"I know that!" she snapped. "Don't you think I know that? I've been listening to it night and day, day and night since he was born! I'm doing the best I can—"

She burst into tears, and Jake felt like a heel. Steve jumped up and took Andy, and April dropped her head against his chest. "Come on, baby, you're just tired,"

he cooed in a voice loud enough to be heard over Andy's screaming.

Jake took the baby, and surprisingly, Andy hushed
instantly. April jerked her head up. "He stopped. What
did you do, Jake?"

Jake was afraid to move. "I don't know."

"You must have done *something*," April cried, tears
beginning to roll faster down her cheeks. "Oh, please
think! I have to know what you did!"

"Honey, calm down," Steve said, holding her close
against him. "Let's take advantage of the quiet. Why
don't you lie down?"

"Because I'm so hungry!" she wailed. "I'm so
hungry that I can't sleep, and I can't eat spaghetti,
and—"

"I'll make her something else," Jake said, keeping
his voice low. "How about macaroni and cheese?"

April only cried harder. "I hate that!"

He opened a cabinet and peered in. "How about a
baked potato?"

"That's not enough!"

He gritted his teeth and tried to remain calm. "How
about two baked potatoes?"

April sighed, rolled her eyes and tried to wipe the
tears away, but they kept coming. "All right."

Jake looked at Steve. "You go ahead and eat, Steve.
I'll take care of this."

April wandered out of the room, still weeping, and
Steve sat back down and began studying his diagram
again as he ate his spaghetti. "Don't worry about her,"
he said. "It's just postpartum depression. It's normal."

"I know," Jake said. "I have it, too."

While Jake held the baby on one shoulder, he prepared the potatoes for the microwave. In fifteen minutes, they were ready to eat, complete with grated cheese melting on them, butter seeping through and a salad on the side. Andy had fallen asleep on his shoulder, but Jake didn't dare put him down for fear the crying would start again. Dismally, he realized he'd do just about anything to keep Andy quiet. "Where's April?" he whispered.

"In there," Steve said.

Cursing under his breath at Steve's unwillingness to help, Jake went into the living room and found April sound asleep on the couch. He looked down at the plate of potatoes in his hand, moaned inwardly and went back into the kitchen. His spaghetti was already too cold to eat.

Miserable, he plopped down in the chair, careful not to disturb the little banshee.

"And I was thinking about painting the living room primary colors. I wonder if Maggie would mind—"

Jake felt something warm trickling down his shirt and looked down to see that Andy had wet all over him. But the baby was still asleep, and the fear of that screaming voice was more intense to Jake than the thought of tolerating the wetness for a while.

Jake closed his eyes and told himself that the night would be over soon.

IT WAS ALMOST MIDNIGHT when April, fed and rested, pulled herself together enough to take over the baby again. Jake, who had managed to get the kitchen cleaned up despite the fact that he had held the sleeping baby for the rest of his stay, couldn't get out of the house fast enough.

He hoped Maggie had gotten in a megadose of studying. He hadn't heard from her all night, and he hadn't called for fear of disturbing her. She was preparing for her first college test, one that he realized might be the most important of her college career. If she did poorly on it, with all the other problems in her life, it might just be the catalyst she needed to give up on school entirely. He had to make sure that didn't happen.

He pulled his bike into his garage and went into the kitchen, confronting the absolute silence there. "Maggie?" he called.

No answer. Worried, he went into the living room, but his worries faded instantly when he saw her sound asleep on the couch, her book and notes scattered across the floor where they had fallen when she'd fallen asleep.

Smiling softly, he went to sit beside her on the couch and leaned over to nuzzle her sleep-warmed neck. "Wake up, sleepyhead," he whispered.

Her eyes cracked open with as much difficulty as if she'd slept all night, and she frowned slightly. "You're back."

"Yep. Did you get a lot of studying done?"

She sat up, suddenly distraught, and looked around at the papers scattered on the floor. "Oh, no. I hardly studied at all. I fell sound asleep...." She got off the couch and began picking up the papers, as if they were scattered pieces of her life. "What am I gonna do?"

"Not at all?" Jake asked. "You didn't study *anything*?"

"I must have looked at it for all of ten minutes before I fell asleep," she said. Her face reddened, and gritting her teeth, she uttered, "Damn, damn, damn!

Now I'll have to stay up for the rest of the night, *if* Andy doesn't."

"Just stay over here and finish studying. April can handle it."

"I can't stay out all night! I have to set some kind of example."

"But your daughter is married, Maggie. What does she care?"

"She cares, okay?" Maggie snapped. She took a deep breath and tried to calm herself. "Look, it'll be all right. I'll just have to take it all home and cram for the rest of the night. It'll probably work out better, anyway. It'll still be fresh on my mind when I take the test."

"But your mind won't be fresh, Maggie. You can't operate without sleep."

"I got sleep, okay? Just now."

"But that's not enough!"

"It's plenty!" she returned. "The test is the most important thing. How can I ever expect to be a psychologist if I flunk my first psychology test?"

Jake threw up his hands and went to his stereo cabinet. "Here. If you can't stay here, take this personal tape player and this jazz sax tape. Go home, lock your bedroom door and put on these headphones to block out the noise, and don't let them interrupt you. Take a pot of coffee in there with you to stay awake, cram all night, and then call in sick at work tomorrow and come over here and crash after the test."

"But April's a basket case, and Steve—"

"Steve needs to grow up," Jake cut in. "Let him do it. Andy's his baby. He needs to get his head out of the clouds and join the real world. But he won't do it until he has to jump without a parachute. You have to start saying no, Maggie."

"I know." She sighed and slid her arms around his waist and laid her head on his chest. "You're right. It's just when you're so exhausted and stressed out, it's hard to see the obvious."

"And the obvious is that it's *your* house and you have a life, too. Help April when you can, but don't take over her responsibilities for her. The sooner she takes responsibility for her own life, the easier things will be for you. I'm telling you, I almost lost my mind over there tonight. April whining, Steve babbling, Andy screaming...I don't know how you can stand it."

Maggie lifted her head from his shoulder, wrinkling her nose. "He wet on you, didn't he?"

"Among other things. I think you should have the doctor check out his stomach, too. He spit up about three thousand times. I smell like sour puke."

Maggie laughed. "That's normal. There's nothing wrong with him."

"Well, it's not normal for me."

The sobriety on Jake's face struck an amused note in Maggie. "You had a terrible night, didn't you?"

"*Terrible* doesn't begin to describe it," Jake said. "Maggie, you've got to do something. You can't go on living like that."

"I know." She sighed. "But I'm sure things'll settle down soon. It's just that this first week is especially hard."

"If you think this week is hard, wait till Steve opens the nursery. You should see some of the crazy ideas he has for transforming your house."

Maggie threw her hands over her ears. "Stop. Don't tell me, because I really can't deal with it right now."

Jake framed her face in his hands and coaxed her to look at him. "Maggie, let me teach you a new word that may not yet be in your vocabulary. It's spelled *N-O. No.* See if you can say it."

Maggie grinned. "I know that word, Jake. I used it on you, remember?"

He matched her grin. "How could I forget? Well, it may not have worked on me, but it can work on parasitic children."

"My daughter's not a parasite," Maggie said defensively. "She just needs a little help."

"Correction," he said. "She needs a lot of help. And she'll keep demanding it until she learns to do without it."

Maggie moaned and pulled herself off of the couch. "I know, Jake, and I appreciate your trying to help. But I can't abandon her with a good conscience just yet. I can't stand to see her struggling, and if I can help, I will. That's what parenthood is all about. Someday you'll see."

He caught the line aimed at the future she saw for him and bristled. "Is that so?"

Maggie gave him a sad smile and picked up her notes and textbook. "Thanks for helping me, Jake. I hope I can repay the favor someday."

He stopped her at the door, cupped her chin and kissed her with sweetness and patience and a warmth that never failed to make her feel cherished. "I love you," he whispered.

She couldn't say it just yet. Admitting her feelings seemed too much of a surrender to what she feared. Love was like a commitment, and a commitment to him would be a betrayal. And she didn't want to do anything that would ultimately hurt him. Or herself.

Maggie touched his face, smiled sweetly at him, then got into her car.

Jake stood in the garage and watched her until she had driven out of sight.

STUDYING ALL NIGHT was an exercise in futility for Maggie. The baby awoke repeatedly throughout the night, and each time, even though April attended to him, Maggie felt the need to help. Steve was often at April's side, however, and Maggie forced herself back to her books, fighting to stay awake.

By the time she took the test, she was so exhausted, she didn't care if she passed or failed. She wound up passing on a C, which made her feel even more defeated, and by the time she met Jake at The Grill, she was ready to crawl into a cocoon and die.

He pulled his key chain out of his pocket, slipped his house key off and dropped it onto the table in front of her. "Call in sick, Maggie, because if you don't, you will be. Then go to my house and sack out. I have one more class this afternoon, and after that I'll be working in my studio, so I won't bother you."

"Really?" Maggie asked, trying not to look so lackluster. "You're sure you don't mind?"

He took her hand and forced her to look at him. "Maggie, I want you there."

"I'm starting to be too much trouble. I can't believe all you had to do for me last night. If I hadn't been so out of it, I wouldn't have let you."

"I can't say I'll volunteer for that again," he admitted, "but I'm not holding it against you."

Maggie offered him a slight grin. "April said you're the only one who can make Andy stop crying."

"That's because everybody else in that house is insane," Jake said. "No offense."

"You think I'm insane?"

"Not yet, but I think your daughter and son-in-law are working hard on driving you to it."

The harsh tone in his voice disheartened her. Maggie dropped her voice, and said, "Maybe so."

"That's why I want you to get some sleep this afternoon. Go right now, crawl into the bed and sleep until the cows come home."

"Well, not that long, but maybe a few hours. You're sure it's all right?"

"I'm sure," he said with a grin. "But beware. I might crawl in there with you when I finish my work."

She smiled. "Then you do have ulterior motives."

"You better believe I do."

His flirtatious smile was enough to carry Maggie all the way to his house, and she went in and sighed at the wonderful peace and quiet. She opened the back door, letting in the cool ocean breeze. The temperature was quickly rising, though there was still a nip in the air. Still, a few scattered sun worshipers lay on the beach, soaking up the last of the season's rays.

Maggie went to Jake's bedroom, slipped under his covers and got comfortable on his pillow. And before she'd had the chance to think how good it felt, she was sound asleep.

THE SOUND OF A KNOCK woke her from her nap, and Maggie looked at the clock and saw that she had been sleeping for two hours. From Jake's bedroom, she could hear the serene sound of the surf against the shore and women's voices speaking softly outside.

The knock came again. Maggie pulled out of bed and straightening her hair, went into the living room. At the back door stood three women in string bikinis, tanned and young, with bodies that would have made any sane man drool. She wondered how they managed to keep goose bumps from marring their oiled skin in the cool wind. Stiffening, she pulled back the screen. "Yes?"

The platinum blonde who seemed to be the ringleader of this string-bikini triad looked a little surprised to see her. "Is Jake here?"

"No, he's—" Maggie's words fell when she heard the sound of the garage door opening and the motorcycle pulling into the garage. "I guess that's him now."

Platinum Blonde waited patiently for Jake to get inside, and while she did, she gave Maggie a critical once-over that made her want to scream. Instead, Maggie kept her mouth shut and feigned the same confidence that the girl exuded, all the while wishing she could grow claws and scratch that smug expression off the blonde's face once and for all.

The door opened and Jake came inside. "Maggie? I thought you were asleep."

"I was."

Maggie stepped back as the three women bopped inside as if they needed no invitation. She stared, astonished, at their tight little rear ends revealed in those bare bathing suits. She had *never* looked like that, even when she was thirteen. The thought made her feel ill.

"Hi, Jake," Platinum said in her best Marilyn Monroe voice. "I didn't realize your mother was here."

Maggie's head shot up, and she glared at the girl.

Jake didn't find it any more amusing than Maggie. "Carol, Maggie's not my mother."

"Oh," she said, spinning around so that Jake could get a good look at her buns. "Sorry."

"No problem," Maggie said, though she didn't yet know how much damage that statement had done to her heart. She'd have to assess that later. Right now she was too busy watching the eye contact from each of the girls to Jake.

Carol turned back around, propped a hand on the counter and struck a pose that made Maggie want to put up her dukes. "We were just looking for a place to get warm."

Jake breathed a mirthless laugh. "Have you tried putting something on, Carol? It works wonders sometimes."

Carol's smile was blatantly seductive. "We didn't bring anything else. Anyway, we were hoping you'd come out and play with us later."

Jake offered a slight grin and flashed Maggie a do-you-believe-this look. "Play with you?"

"Yeah, you know. We could throw a Frisbee or swim a little."

Anything to make you bounce and glisten? Maggie thought as she turned to leave the room. It was time for her to leave.

"Maggie, where're you going?" Jake asked.

She shrugged. "To get my things. I have to get home."

Carol grinned. "Gee, I hope we aren't interrupting anything."

Jake bristled and made no attempt to hide it. "Carol, I appreciate the invitation, but I have plans for the afternoon. I'm spending it with Maggie."

Maggie hesitated at the door and turned back to the girls.

Carol erased the distance between them and took Jake's arm, making sure her breast mashed against it.

Her disproportionately large breast.

Her barely covered breast.

"Come on, Jake. We've all been missing you. You've been hiding away for too long."

"I've been busy," he said, retrieving his arm and stepping back. He sent Maggie an uncomfortable look again.

"Please, Jake," one of the other girls said. Maggie glanced at her bare bun and noticed the tattoo of a heart on it. She couldn't wait until the woman got old and withered and that heart began to droop. The thought almost made her feel better.

"Not today," Jake said, walking back to the door, offering them a cue to leave.

Reluctantly, the girls left, but not before Carol put her arms around his neck and pressed her fig-leaf-covered pelvis against his. "I miss you, Jake."

He took her arms and pulled her away from him. "I appreciate the sentiment, Carol."

Then not giving her another chance to grab him, he closed the screen between them.

When the trio had gone down the steps of his deck to the beach, Jake turned back to Maggie. "Sorry about that."

"Don't worry about it." Maggie turned away and went to the kitchen, desperately trying to hide the turmoil on her face. "You should have gone. It's a beautiful day."

She felt him watching her and she wanted to cry, but she wouldn't allow herself to. Their days were numbered and it was good that he had a couple hundred tight-bodied beauties to fall back on. She should be thankful.

"You're upset."

Maggie breathed a mirthless laugh. "I'm not. It's just...those bathing suits. I thought those were against the law or something."

"Not here, they're not. Carol likes for people to look at her."

"No kidding." Maggie busied herself filling a glass with water, and he reached out for her hand and pulled her against him.

"Really," she said, trying hard not to melt. "Go on out. It won't bother me at all."

"Not at all?" Jake teased. "Not even a little? Not even if I wear my thong bathing suit, too?"

"You have one of those?"

He laughed and nuzzled her neck. "Of course not. I was just trying to get you going. Mmm, you're warm. Did you get enough sleep?"

"I guess," she said, peering past him to the girls frolicking on the beach beneath the window, trying hard to catch his attention again.

"Well, I could use some. How about lying back down with me?"

As much as Maggie wanted to make love to Jake now, her heart wasn't in it. There was no way she'd reveal her body to him ten minutes after he'd witnessed *the Carol*. "I'd probably better get home," she said. "I really need to—"

"No way." His tone held a strong note of finality. "You're staying here. I can't let you go back to that until you've had enough sleep. Come on. Just lie down with me and let me hold you. I won't try to jump your bones or anything. I just want you to sleep."

She smiled up at him and thought of the alternative. He could be frolicking on the beach with those women, and he chose to hold her while she slept. How could she say no? "All right," she whispered. "I guess I am still tired."

"Of course, you are. It takes more than two hours to make up for two nights of lost sleep."

He pulled her into the bedroom, climbed into bed with her and pulled her against him.

Wrapped in his arms and legs, Maggie fell into the deepest and most relaxing sleep she had ever experienced in her life. And for a while, it was as if nothing could intrude on their world—not children or nurseries or bare-bunned babes. For Jake was her fortress.

Chapter Twelve

"Where in the world did Steve find all these kids?" Jake asked a week later as they stood in the center of the living room with fifteen kids, thirty parents and the photographers from the newspaper Steve had somehow coerced into coming for the "Grand Opening Celebration" to acclimate the children to the nursery before it opened.

"From Mrs. Dot's Preschool and Forgery Emporium," Maggie said deadpan.

"What?"

"That woman who was indicted for forgery last week. Steve hung out in her parking lot passing out flyers." She heard something crash in the kitchen and handed Andy to Jake. "Oh, my God, what's that?"

Jake followed Maggie into the kitchen, where they found Alex, a two-year-old with a perpetual runny nose and a talent for mountain climbing. Since there were no mountains in sight, he had decided Maggie's counters would do. The stool he had used to get from the floor to the countertop had fallen over, but not before he'd scaled the counter and opened the cabinet, where he was perusing the contents.

"Alex!" Maggie rushed forward and grabbed the child before he sent a dozen cans tumbling down on himself.

He wrestled her as she set him down, then grabbed the stool, set it upright and began to climb again. "No, Alex. You can't do this!"

"I'm hungry." Still wrestling Alex, Maggie turned around to see Sarah, a three-year-old who rarely took her thumb from her mouth, staring up at her with big eyes.

"We just had cake, Sarah. Yours is still on your plate in the living room."

"But I want something else."

"We don't have anything else."

Andy began to cry, despite the fact that Jake was holding him, and Maggie threw Jake a despairing look.

The whine that wound from Sarah's throat was more grating than a dentist's drill. "I want candy!"

Maggie let Alex go and went to quiet Sarah before her parents heard the ruckus and decided that their child wouldn't be happy here. Which wouldn't be such a bad thing, she told herself, but if Steve and April were really going to do this, she didn't want to be accused of sabotaging their effort.

Alex got away and began climbing the stool again as Sarah sent her dramatics into high gear and fell to the floor, where her fit could take full bloom.

Jake grabbed Alex with one arm and set him down again. Andy screamed louder.

"Damn!" Jake shouted. "What is it with these kids!"

April burst into the kitchen and daggered Jake with a disparaging look. "Would you mind not cursing in front of the children? The parents can hear!"

"Sorry," Jake said, "but this is a madhouse. You don't seriously think you can handle this eight hours a day!"

Sarah screamed two octaves louder, and April picked her up and told her something about goody bags with candy being handed out in the other room. The girl stopped crying instantly and scurried out of the room.

"Now, what's *his* problem?" April asked, referring to Alex, who was yelling and fighting to get back onto the stool.

"He needs a good spanking, that's what," Jake said, bouncing Andy and trying to make him hush.

April wrestled the two-year-old from Maggie and stooped down to confront him. "Alex, do you want to climb?"

The boy screamed out that he did, and April tried again. "All right, then. Come in here and I'll show you something you *can* climb."

"What?" Maggie asked suspiciously. "I don't want him climbing the bookshelves. And don't let him get on the furniture. Some of it is antique."

"Don't worry, Mom," April said. "I'm going to distract him. Chill out. And see if you can do something about Andy."

Maggie searched the counter for a spare pacifier. One was sitting in a bowl of things she had sterilized earlier. "Here, Andy," she said, putting it in his mouth. "Is that better?"

The baby stopped crying, and Jake seemed to relax a little. "Maggie, this is a nightmare. How are you gonna live in all this? How will you get any studying done?"

Maggie plopped down in a chair and shook her head. "I don't know. But I'll manage, somehow. I've just got to try to relax and not get all upset—"

"Ms. Conrad?" a voice asked from the doorway.

Maggie looked up. "Yes?"

"Are you the Grandma that Grandma's House was named after?"

Maggie came to her feet. "I guess so. I own the house."

A camera flashed at her, and Maggie reached up to self-consciously touch her hair.

"I'm Sid Greenly from the *Times*. Steven and I used to be neighbors, and I came as a favor to him. Do you mind if I ask you a few questions for the article on the grand opening?"

Maggie struggled not to show the dread on her face. "Of course not."

"What part will you play in this day-care center?" he asked, already jotting on his notepad.

"What part?" Maggie repeated. "Well...none. I just live here. I think my daughter and son-in-law—"

"None?" The man looked up from his notepad and shook his head with disapproval. "If you don't mind my saying so, Ms. Conrad, I wouldn't say that if I were you. It isn't good PR."

"PR?" she asked. "What do you mean?"

"I mean, the whole concept of this place is that it's homey and cozy and secure, just like Grandma's house. If I write that Grandma isn't even going to be here, it won't help you much."

"Oh..." Maggie looked helplessly at Jake, then back at the reporter, who seemed to be looking her over with a deep frown on his face. "Then...don't say that. Put that I'll be overseeing the operation, even though my daughter and her husband will be doing the day-to-day things...."

The camera flashed again, and the reporter reached out to stop the photographer. "No more pictures," he said. "We can't use them."

"Why not?" the photographer asked.

"Because she looks too young. If we print a picture of her as Grandma, nobody'll believe it." He gestured toward her hair. "Couldn't you pull it back a little, put on a pair of glasses and change into a more conservative dress instead of those tight slacks?"

Maggie gaped at him. "No, I couldn't."

"I'm just telling you it'll be better PR if you look the part—"

"Wait a minute." Jake stepped forward, still holding the baby, whose head bobbed against his shoulder. "Since when do reporters care what kind of PR a business has?"

"I just want my story to be more interesting," the man said. "I have to have something to hang this on or it's not newsworthy. The grandma in Grandma's house was newsworthy, but not if she looks so young. Who are *you*, anyway?"

Jake seemed to bristle at the question. "I'm her—her—"

"My friend," Maggie threw in.

"Friend? As in boyfriend?" the reporter asked, his face brightening. "Hey, this might not work for the day-care, but we're doing a piece in a few weeks on older women dating younger men. I just got a great idea for an angle. Grandma's Guy. Or even better, something to do with the Oedipus complex."

"The Oedipus complex?" Jake blurted out.

"Yeah. We could explore why you would go for a grandmother in the first place."

"Look at her," Jake said through his teeth. "It's obvious why I go for her."

"Does she look at all like your mother?"

Jake gritted his teeth tighter, and Maggie stared at him in horror. "Maggie, if I break this man's neck and throw him in the ditch behind your yard, do you think it'll destroy the PR for Grandma's House?"

"Probably," she said.

"Good." He handed the baby to her, then started toward the reporter.

"Hey, wait a minute! I didn't mean to offend anyone."

"Get out," Jake said, pointing to the back door. "And take your photographer with you."

"But the article..."

"We don't *need* an article," Jake said. "Steve's already signed up three more kids than he needs! What the hell does he need publicity for?"

"It never hurts to open with a bang."

"We'll open with a bang, all right," Jake said. "But it'll be the sound of your body hitting the pavement when I throw your ass out of this yard. Do you understand what I'm saying?"

"Damn, you're touchy," Greenly said, stuffing his notepad into his pocket and scurrying out the door. "You can forget being in my older woman–younger man article. I'll just find someone else."

"I'll try to live with that," Jake said before he slammed the door behind him.

He turned around and glared at Maggie. "I hope you know you live in a madhouse. And it's only gonna get worse."

"Yes," she said, struggling between the conflicting urges to burst into tears or burst out laughing. She wasn't sure which way her emotions would swing. "I do know that."

"I hope you also know that my sanity has always been something I've prided myself in, and I'm not ready to surrender it just yet."

Her mouth cracked into a smile. "Yes. I suspected that."

"Then you'll understand why I'm going to walk out of here right now, get on my bike and ride like the wind before I really do break someone's neck."

"Yes," she said as laughter edged up in her throat. "That's fine."

"And I hope you realize that I really like you sane, too."

"Why?" she asked, unable to control her laughter any longer. "Is your mother sane?"

"Now and then," he said, not catching Maggie's laughter. "But as you know, that's where the similarities end." Jake watched her laugh for a moment, then shaking his head, he started for the door. "I'll see you later. When things settle down, I'll be back."

"All right. See you later, Ed."

He cracked a grin and opened the door. "Later, Mom."

After he had gone, Maggie laughed till her sides ached, but as the laughter died out, she realized that the situation really wasn't all that funny. The activities at her home had been more than Jake could take, and her problems had run him away. And if that wasn't enough, his very interest in her had been turned into the suggestion of something dirty.

Maggie wondered why she had ever laughed about it at all.

Maybe it was that sanity thing, she told herself. Maybe she was losing it already. Maybe she would be the last person to know she had snapped.

But as she watched April and Steve herding the children and parents out to the backyard to see the equipment Steve had put together into a toddler's paradise, she realized that she couldn't snap just yet. There was too much to do, and it was highly possible that she would be the last thinking person to hold it all together.

OEDIPUS COMPLEX! Jake recalled the reporter's stupid observation again and felt his face reddening. The only saving grace to it all was that the man would be too angry to write the article.

Jake pulled into his garage and went straight to his studio, where he'd been pounding out most of his emotions in a lump of clay. It was closer to looking the way he wanted, although the look on the face in the clay changed from day to day. One day it was sad, the next laughing, the next perplexed....

Daily, he changed the cast of the lines on the face— lines that he thought gave it character and class, lines that made it constantly changing and always unpredictable. And the eyes ... those were the hardest. Capturing the intelligence, the life, the joy...

He thought of Maggie laughing after the reporter had insulted them both. He would have expected her to cry. She had taken it better than he but he knew it had hurt her down to her core, down past what those eyes revealed.

Still, he couldn't escape the foundation of happiness always lurking in those eyes and that smile that always seemed to be on the verge of laughter. If he could just get it right.

The doorbell rang. Reluctant to leave the clay, Jake wiped his hands and went to the door.

Carol stood there, once again wearing her thong bikini, though the temperature had dropped twenty degrees. Her tan was impeccable, but he could only imagine what she'd look like in ten years. She'd be a prune. Only women like Maggie, who had better things to do than bask in the sun twelve hours a day, were able to age beautifully.

"Hi, Jake."

"How's it going, Carol?"

"Pretty good." She stepped inside, uninvited, and ran her hand up Jake's chest. "I've missed you."

"So you said the other day."

She slid her hand up to his face and stroked a thumb across his mouth. "But you were distracted then. Your mother was here...."

He took her hands and pulled her away from him. "She's not my mother."

"Jake, you can't be serious about her. We used to have so much fun together. She must be at least thirty-five...."

Jake grinned. "At least. I've really enjoyed this little visit, Carol, but I've been in the studio working—"

"Let me watch."

"No, I don't think so. Why don't you just run along? Surely you can find *somebody* else to play with."

Her expression collapsed into hurt, but it didn't faze him at all. "You've changed, Jake."

"Damn right, I have, darlin'." With that, he urged her out the door, then closed it behind her.

He went back to the studio and studied the face he was working on again. It wasn't easy, he thought. It was the hardest piece he'd ever done, and he wasn't sure he was up to it.

But that was only natural, he thought. He had the same mixed emotions about Maggie, herself. His relationship with her was the hardest he'd ever had, and he wasn't sure he was up to it. But worse than that, he wasn't sure if Maggie was.

The alternative, however, was the worst scenario of all.

Chapter Thirteen

"I'm not up to this." Maggie muttered the words into the mirror of her bathroom, where she had just found Alex straddling the sink and "coloring" on the glass with her favorite lipstick. "I'm being punished and I don't know what for."

She heard the sound of Alex screaming from the living room—over the sound of fourteen other chattering children and a Sesame Street record playing "Put Down the Ducky" in the background—and told herself that the sooner she got her makeup on and left for school, the sooner her headache would go away. It had only been a week since the day-care center had opened, but it seemed the parents brought the kids earlier each day and picked them up later. From their temperaments and demanding personalities, she didn't blame their folks one bit.

And then there were her studies, which were failing badly. She got home before the children were gone each day and found herself "helping out" with Andy as Steve and April wound up the day. And then, after the house was quiet again—except for Andy's sporadic crying jags—she found that April was "too dead" to attend to her own child and expected her mother to

cook supper, bathe Andy and clean up if she wanted a
place to sit. The only thing that had made Maggie do
those things was her need to eat, her need to stop
smelling sour milk on her grandson and her need to
avoid killing herself walking through the living room.

"Mom!" April's voice bellowed out of the living
room and Maggie abandoned her eye shadow and went
to see what disaster had befallen her house now.

"What is it?"

"Andy," April said. "His diaper needs changing,
and Steve and I are right in the middle of finger painting."

Maggie glanced around at the children elbow-deep
in blue paint—a color that would absolutely clash with
her green sofa and off-white carpet—and moaned inwardly. As organized as it all seemed—and as compe-
tent as Steve and April appeared with the children—she
didn't doubt for a minute that tonight she'd be scrubbing the paint off of something.

She picked Andy up out of his car seat on the floor
and cooing softly to him, took him to change him. She
knew she was being taken advantage of in a big way,
but it would be unfair to let little Andy suffer from his
parents' irresponsibility. The moment she took off his
diaper, he sent a spray arcing up over her blouse. Miserably, she looked down at herself.

"You did that on purpose, didn't you? Because you
knew I was in a hurry and didn't have time to change.
You want me to stay here with you, don't you, to res-
cue you from this loony bin you're a part of all day."

Andy smiled and cooed back at her.

She finished changing his diaper, then took him back
into the living room to put him into his seat.

"Mom? Do you have another minute?"

Maggie swung around. "No, April, I don't. I have to be at school in fifteen minutes, and now I have to find something else to wear because Andy sprayed my shirt."

Steve beamed. "That's my boy."

"But I need another pair of hands. Heather's getting paint all over the—"

April cut off her words when she saw the paint can tip over and a puddle of blue paint spill onto the floor.

Muttering a curse under her breath, Maggie grabbed a towel, dropped to her knees and began scrubbing it up.

The doorbell rang. Maggie cursed again. Andy began crying, and the noise level increased twenty decibels.

"Come in," Steve shouted. The door opened and Jake stepped inside.

Maggie gave him a doleful look. "Jake, what are you doing here?"

"You were supposed to meet me for breakfast," he said. "What happened?"

"Breakfast?" She slapped her forehead, getting blue paint on her bangs. "I forgot. I'm sorry, Jake. It's just been so crazy—"

Jake took the rag out of her hands and wiped the paint from her face. "Here, let me take care of this. You're gonna be late for class."

"Thank you. I have to change my blouse, and I haven't finished my makeup—"

"Mom, help!"

Maggie swung around to see Alex climbing the couch with blue hands, and she screamed, "Alex, no!"

"I'll handle it," Jake said, grabbing the boy. "Go get ready. Hurry!"

"But they're ruining my house!"

"Mom, I'm sorry, but I'm trying not to let this happen."

Maggie hesitated, and Jake pointed a decisive finger toward the bedroom. "Go, Maggie. I'll take care of this."

Maggie went back to her room, washed the blue paint from her hands and bangs and slapped on the rest of her makeup. Viciously, she pulled off her blouse and grabbed the first thing she could find to put on in its place.

In the living room, she heard Jake yell, "All right, everybody freeze! Don't anybody move!"

Maggie listened to Steve's objections as she buttoned her blouse, then wiping her face, she ventured out of her room.

Jake had a stack of towels and was covering the carpet and sofas with them. "As soon as I get out of class today, I'm gonna find some plastic for you to put down when you have to do asinine projects like this. Something to cover the couches, too, as much as I hate plastic covers. Maggie worked too hard for all this to have it destroyed in one week."

"Jake, we're trying to keep it clean," April whined. "We're doing our best."

"Your best obviously isn't good enough," Jake said, wiping the last of the paint from the couch. It looked as if it might dry unscathed. Maggie breathed a sigh of relief.

Jake looked up and saw her, and his face softened instantly. "You okay, babe?"

She made a poor attempt at smiling. "Yeah. I'd better hurry."

"You wanna ride?"

"No, I'd better take the car."

"Oh, Maggie, the car ran out of gas just as I coasted into the driveway last night," Steve said. "I was planning on walking to the gas station during nap time."

Maggie closed her eyes and gritted her teeth. "Can you bring me home to get my car after class today, Jake?"

"No problem." Despite his accommodation, he fired Steve a disgusted look for taking advantage of Maggie again. Steve didn't notice.

"All right." She grabbed her purse and looked around at her house again and told herself it was futile to worry about it now. All she could hope was that it would survive until she got home.

Jake walked her out and handed her her helmet. "Did you eat?"

"Of course not," she said. "I have a knot the size of Nebraska in my stomach and a headache that makes a good case for euthanasia."

He leaned over and kissed her, and at once she felt the tension seeping out of her by degrees. "Feel better," he whispered.

She smiled. "I do now."

But as they rode to the campus, Maggie realized that her life was out of control and somehow, if it was the last thing she did, she would get things in order again.

All she had to do was figure out how.

"EXCUSE ME, MS. CONRAD. I hate to disturb you, but..."

Maggie jumped and looked around the classroom she had come into an hour ago and saw that the students were filing out. She had known the minute she sat down next to the wall that it was a mistake. It was too comfortable, leaning her head back that way, allowing her eyes to close a little longer than a blink required.

And now Professor Anthony Moore was frowning down at her, the communion of his eyebrows making her feel as if she'd done something dreadfully wrong.

"Uh . . . I must have dozed off. . . ."

"Yes, you must have," he said. "Perhaps you wouldn't mind sleeping at home from now on. I realize that Shakespeare can sometimes be construed as boring by those with a less intelligent mind, but I'd prefer not to have my lectures tainted with sleeping students."

Maggie realized she was the only student left in the classroom and came to her feet. "I—I'm so sorry. It'll never happen again. I promise. Really, I don't know what came over me." As she spoke, she realized he had insulted her intelligence, and rallying, she snapped up her chin. "As for my intelligence, *sir,* I have as much as one can cultivate when she doesn't have a quiet moment all day long."

"Perhaps you should restructure your life, Ms. Conrad, if you, indeed, plan to accommodate a college education."

"You know, that's a terrific idea," she said, sarcasm dripping on her voice. "And I think I'll start today."

Gathering her books, she stormed from the room, desperately trying not to cry in front of the man who seemed to have taken such pleasure in calling her down. But how could she blame him, she asked herself. He had no way of knowing what hell her life had been the past few days. And why should he even care? He wasn't there to help problem-plagued students stay awake in class.

The anger and humiliation threatened to choke her. She was a grown woman, and it was time she figured out how to act like one.

Turning a corner, she ran headlong into Jake, who was waiting for her. Her books tumbled to the floor and he bent down to get them.

"Maggie, we've got to stop meeting like this."

When she didn't laugh, he stood up and stacked her books together with his own. Maggie reached out to take them back.

"Maggie, what's wrong?"

"I fell asleep in class, *that's* what's wrong!" she whispered viciously, starting to walk again. He fell into step with her. "I missed the whole lecture. I might as well not have come. It would have been better if I hadn't. Now he thinks I'm an idiot."

"Maggie, it happens. It's not that big a deal."

She spun around, her eyes livid. "Not that big a deal? How can you say that? Have you ever fallen asleep in class?"

"Well . . . no. But I've yawned a couple hundred times. Does that count?"

"Damn it, Jake, this isn't funny!" She started walking again, her jaw clenched.

"Maggie, hold on. You're really upset, aren't you?"

She shook her head and waved him off with her free hand. "I don't want to talk about it anymore."

"Maggie, you're just tired. What other class do you have today?"

"Philosophy. And I'm just not up to Plato and Eugene right now."

"Plato I've heard of, but who's Eugene?"

"Nobody," she said. "My professor. He'll probably catch me snoozing in his class and come up with some profound philosophical comparison that he'll want to share with me later, which I'd rather be hung up by my toenails and beaten than have to listen to.''

"So he's the one you went out with," Jake said quietly. "I figured he was. You've always seemed so interested in that class."

Again, she turned on him. "Interested? Jake, I'm interested in all my classes. That's why I'm here. To learn whatever I can get anyone to teach me! But there are too many obstacles, too many hurdles. And I'm running out of energy!"

"What you need to run out of is patience," he said. "With your daughter and her husband."

"What about you?" she snapped.

Jake took a step back and frowned down at her. "Me? What did I do?"

Maggie shook her head, as if he could never understand in a million years, and started walking again. "Nothing. You're right. I'm just tired, and if I keep on with this, I'll say something I'll regret."

"Like what?" he asked, his tone growing angrier by the moment.

"Leave it alone, Jake," she said. "I'm not in the mood."

"No, I won't leave it alone. This has to do with me. Tell me what the hell you're talking about."

"It has nothing to do with you," Maggie insisted. "I just need some rest and some quiet time to study, but I'm not likely to get it anytime soon. And it makes me angry. Real, real angry."

"At me?"

"At the whole world."

They walked in silence for a moment as the anger flourished like a disease within her. Could she really be angry at the whole world, or just at those in her life who had tugged her away from her dream? Maybe she just needed to be more focused, Maggie told herself. Maybe she just needed to be more stubborn about being distracted from it.

They reached the building where her philosophy class was held, and she slowed her step. "Well, I'll see you later."

Jake caught her arm. "Maggie, you're not going to your philosophy class today. You're coming home with me until you have to go to work."

"Excuse me?"

"You need a nap," he said. "You can borrow someone's notes tomorrow."

"Jake, I have to go to class."

"Why? Will Eugene be disappointed if you don't show?"

Her teeth clamped together. "No. I have to go because I'm committed to all of my classes."

"So committed that you fall asleep?"

Fire climbed up Maggie's neck and reddened her face, and she focused her furious eyes on Jake. "I'm doing the best I can."

"You're doing more than your best, Maggie. You're doing way more than any one human can handle, and that's why you're coming home with me."

"Damn it, Jake, I'm not!"

She turned away and covered her face, where tears were beginning to fall faster. Her hand trembled visibly. There had to be some way of getting control, she thought, but she was like a marionette with a string on every limb, taking orders from everyone in her life and being what everyone needed her to be. The perfect mother, the perfect grandmother, the perfect student, the perfect girlfriend . . .

"Maggie, what's the matter with you?" Jake asked, lowering his voice.

"What's the matter with me?" Maggie repeated, rage wavering in her voice. "I'll tell you what's the matter with me. You're trying to control me just like April and Steve. You're trying to manipulate me into being whatever it is you need, but nobody gives a damn about what I need. You know what I need right now, Jake? A college education, that's what. And I'm not going to let you or anybody else stand in my way of that."

It was the first time she had seen fire climb Jake's cheeks, and she knew he was even more angry now than he'd been when he'd discovered her lie about April. "Maggie, you're walking on thin ice. I'm not gonna stand here and let you hurl accusations at me. I know you're just tired and you're not thinking before you talk—"

"I've done nothing *but* think in the last few days!" she cried. "I've let you mislead me. I've let you make me believe in those sand castles you turn out by the dozens."

"So what?" he asked. "I believe in them, too."

"No, you don't," she cried. "You never have. You know how easily they can crumble, and I should know that, too. After all, it was a crumbling sand castle that brought us together."

"Maggie, just because sand castles can be knocked down doesn't mean you can't rebuild them."

"But what if you run out of sand!" she cried. "What if someone comes along and vacuums it all up!"

The humor in her words would have struck him if not for the rage and agony in her face as she shouted them.

"Maggie, there's always enough sand for a dream."

"But sometimes there's not enough glue to hold it all together," she whispered. "Sometimes the wind and the waves are just too strong, so you have to do everything in your power to keep it standing. Even if it means making sacrifices that will save you from hurting later. Even if it means facing things you don't want to face."

"What things?"

"Things like how wrong this whole relationship is, about how I'm holding you back, about how you're holding me back, about how I'm going to get over the pain when your little game is over and you realize what it means to date a woman ten years your senior."

A breath issued from his lungs as though he'd been walloped in the stomach, and he stood gaping at her, disbelieving. "You think this is a game?"

"I don't know what it is, Jake. All I know is—"

"And when I told you I love you, was that part of the game?" His voice was growing harsher.

She shook her head. "Jake, that's not what I meant—"

"So you think because I'm a few years younger than you, that I don't know what I want?"

"Jake, this is getting—"

Jake grabbed her shoulder and glared into her eyes. "Well, I do know what I want, Maggie, and right now, it's to ram my fist through something again. You have a way of making me want to do that, you know it? So I'm gonna walk away from here and let you go sit in your philosophy class, because I wouldn't dream of letting my concern for your health interfere with your godforsaken education! The control's all yours, Maggie. I'm outta here."

He let go of her roughly, then stormed off across the lawn. And as she watched him go, Maggie felt only weary numbness. But the pain was there, lurking in the shadows, waiting to ambush her when she let her guard down. So she vowed not to let it down. There wasn't time for the tears she felt renewing themselves in her eyes. There was only time for strength—and for decisions and actions that would get her life in order.

Otherwise, she would lose her mind altogether. She was quite sure she'd already lost Jake.

THAT AFTERNOON AFTER WORK, Maggie stopped her car halfway up the driveway of her house, got out and reached for the sign and hammer she had put in the back seat. With her mouth set and her chin held high, she marched to the center of the yard—just in front of the sign that said Grandma's House—jabbed her sign's stake into the dirt and hammered it in farther.

She was standing back, admiring it, when the front door opened. "Mom? What are you doing?"

"Putting a For Sale sign in *my* yard," she said.

"What? You can't!" April turned back inside and shouted, "Steve, come quick!"

Maggie leaned against the sign, fighting the smug smile taking over her face as Steve barreled out the door. "Maggie, are you crazy? We just started a business here. You can't sell this house!"

"Oh, yes, I can," she said, starting toward the door. "It is *my* house, after all. *My* name's on the deed."

"But, Maggie, what about April and me? What about little Andy?"

Maggie laughed softly under her breath as she recognized the play for sympathy. "Little Andy has a mother and a father who are both gainfully employed now. There's no reason you can't find another place to have your nursery. Probably even a place much better than this."

"But the overhead! The cost would eat us up. We'd have to pay rent, buy food—"

Maggie swung around, her eyes suddenly livid. "And what the hell do you think *I* have to do? Do you think money grows in that fungus stuff you have growing in that cup in your bedroom? It doesn't, Steve. I make the same amount whether I'm supporting one person or four people."

"But, Maggie, we were gonna pay you rent as soon as we got on our feet. We were gonna help you out—"

"You were also going to find your own place to live, which seems to have been conveniently forgotten now that you've turned my home into a children's asylum."

"But, Mom!" April's tone suggested oncoming tears, and Maggie started into the house.

"I have some studying to do, April. I suggest you and Steve spend some time discussing what you're going to do. I expect to start showing the house tomorrow. We could even have it sold within a month."

"But, Mom, how could you be so selfish?"

The words were like a spear through Maggie's back, and she flung around and glared at her daughter. "Let me tell you something, April," she said, pointing her finger in her daughter's face. "I have spent the last eighteen years dreaming of getting a college education and becoming a psychologist. There was never any money or any time until just recently, but in the last few weeks, I've seen that slipping through my fingers. You call me selfish? Well, I could be less selfish and quit school, I suppose, and go back to work full-time so I could afford the extra costs around here that neither of you are contributing to. Or I could keep struggling like I am, with no sleep and no privacy, and watch my grades drop until I flunk all my classes. But guess what? I'm sick of not being selfish. You're an adult, April, and it's time you started acting like one. And you'll never do it until I start thinking of myself for a change."

"Jake put you up to this, didn't he?" April shouted. "He told you to do this!"

Maggie's face twisted in confusion. "How could you say that?"

"Because you never acted like this until he came around," April cried. "You started trying to be some young thing with her whole life ahead of her, trying to forget that you have a whole life behind you that includes me."

"I'm not forgetting any of what I've accomplished," Maggie returned. "But that doesn't mean I have to be a slave to it, either. It's time for us both to move forward, April. And Jake has nothing at all to do with that."

She started from the room, but before she was out, April flung out her last stinging barb. "If you didn't spend so much time with him, maybe you'd be doing better in school. Steve and I aren't the only ones to blame, you know."

"Well, you don't have to worry," Maggie said, her voice noticeably weaker. "Because Jake's out of the picture now."

And before her daughter could drill her further, Maggie slammed herself into her bedroom.

The tears came before she'd even reached her bed, and she felt her soul being torn out in great fragments that she feared would never heal again. It wasn't supposed to have happened this way, she thought. She wasn't supposed to have driven Jake away. But her fears had turned their breakup into a self-fulfilling prophecy, and it was her own fault.

She buried her face in her pillow to muffle her sobs, and thought of calling him, begging him to forgive her for the cruel things she'd said, but some stubborn part of her couldn't do it. It was best, she told herself. Right now, as she shook off all the extra baggage in her life, was the best time to end things with Jake, as well. There was no point in prolonging what was inevitable.

Wilted and weary to her heart, she tried to sort through all the changes she was making in her life. She would sell the house, forcing April and Steve to move their day-care center somewhere else. They would get their own place to live, now that they had a nice income, and she would rent an apartment. A small one-bedroom apartment.

She would use the proceeds from the sale of her house to live on until she finished school, and that way she could devote herself completely to her education. Then her life would be almost in order.

Except that she'd be alone.

Funny, she thought, as new tears burned her raw eyes. Today she had too many people in her life, but one by one she was alienating each of them. Some by choice, others not. It didn't matter how it happened. Alone was still alone.

But she'd dealt with aloneness before, and there had been a time, not so long ago, when she had considered solitude a friend. Now it was a threatening enemy, she told herself, but she would fight the battle with it and win. She would learn to live with it again.

But as sleep filtered over her like a tranquilizing drug, she found herself realizing that she'd never before had anyone to compare her solitude to. Until she had met Jake, she had been her own best company. Now she knew the sweet exhilaration of having his arms around her, of feeling his lips graze her skin, of knowing the adoration in his eyes as he smiled at her....

Solitude would never satisfy her again, she thought. And she had no one to blame but herself.

Chapter Fourteen

The chin wasn't tilted just right, Jake thought as his hands worked over the clay face again. It wasn't proud enough. It almost looked defeated, in a rebellious, angry sort of way, and he wouldn't tolerate that on something he cared about.

Over the past three weeks, he had worked at the face night and day, smoothing and caressing and sculpting it into his perception of the way it should be. It should have beauty with dignity, he thought, and the eyes should show a deep compassion mixed with intelligence. A fear of pain. A fragility that offset the pride he wanted to capture.

He wondered if Maggie even knew how complex she was.

His despair at trying—and still failing—to get her clay chin just right overwhelmed him, and unable to work on it anymore, he turned away from the face.

Behind him, on another table, stood the small, intricately created sand castle he had started making the day of their fight. Since then, it had gotten more detailed and precise, redefining the previously reached boundaries of the art he was able to create with sand.

The castle reminded him of her. It was substantive yet fragile, complex yet simple.

He had finished the castle yesterday, and now he didn't want it. It reminded him too much of her. On some level deep beneath his thoughts, he supposed he had always intended to give it to her. Had he thought she would come back to him by now? he asked himself. Had he honestly thought that she would miss him?

Beginning a week after their fight, when he'd decided that he didn't want to face another day without her, Jake had begun trying to call her. Maggie had avoided him completely, which did a lot to make him doubt she had any of the feelings he'd believed she had. And why not? he wondered. She had never claimed to feel that much for him. It was probably easier for her to forget him.

He wished he knew her secret, for as hard as he'd tried, he couldn't get her out of his heart. Her scent hung in all of his clothes, her touch tingled at his fingertips, her taste teased at his mouth.

Other women pranced by, making grand plays for his attention, but he couldn't even see them. He feared he would never feel the same way about any other woman. Why should he, after all, when he'd never felt it before? And if Maggie was truly out of his life, did that mean he was destined to be alone for the rest of it?

On some level, he wished he'd never met her. But on another, much deeper in his heart, he was thankful for the sunshine she'd brought into his life, no matter how brief.

It was the finality he couldn't deal with. The nonsensical reasoning behind it. The fight that—in hindsight—looked like part of a script written to fulfill her own plans.

He sat down and rubbed his face with his hands, and decided he'd have to pull himself together. With or without Maggie, his life had to go on. And he had to do the best he could with it.

But knowing that she wanted him out of her life wasn't good enough. There must be some way to convince her to come back, he thought. There must be some way to get through to her.

THE BOX ARRIVED at Maggie's office a week later, carefully padded and wrapped, but without a card. Her first thought was that it was something Steve had ordered for the nursery—though she couldn't imagine why he would have it sent to her office—and she set it aside, planning to open it at home. Her heart wasn't up for any new surprises, especially if they had to do with Grandma's House. Besides, her concentration at work had decreased tremendously lately, and she told herself it had nothing at all to do with Jake. It was simply that she knew she'd be quitting her job as soon as her house sold and her level of commitment to her work had dropped drastically. If she wanted to keep the job until then, she had no time for opening Steve's packages or daydreaming about what might have been.

But it wasn't easy, she thought, trying to concentrate on the column of numbers she was adding. It seemed to get worse each day. Jake was the first thought that crossed her mind in the morning, and walking across campus, she sought him out, hoping for a glimpse of him, even though she had learned different ent routes to her classes to keep *from* running into him.

Driving down the road, her heart jumped at every motorcycle she saw, and at night, when she locked herself in her room for a few minutes of quiet before Andy's marathon crying jags began, she couldn't stop thinking of Jake's arms around her, the shape of his chest beneath her cheek, the feel of the stubble on his jaw.

She stayed at work late that day, until she had finished what she needed to accomplish, then drove home, dreading what awaited her—another night of chaos and bedlam; another night of slavery; another night of sleeplessness. Her only consolation was that it would all be over soon, if one of those prospects for the house came through.

She brought the box in with her, the box that she hadn't had the heart to open, and set it on the counter. There was something wrong, she thought. The house was too quiet. And the smell . . .

Instead of sour milk, Play-Doh and tempera paint, she smelled a roast cooking in the oven, vegetables steaming and the sound of Yanni playing on the stereo in the next room. Flabbergasted, she went in.

"Hi, Mom," April said from the place where she was curled up with Steve on the couch as the two of them pored over a catalogue of the latest child-care equipment. Little Andy sat contentedly in his swing, a recent discovery that had been worth a million dollars to Maggie.

Maggie gaped at the scene with disbelief. "Who are you and what have you done with my family?"

April giggled. "Oh, Mom. You're so dramatic. We're just getting used to the routine, that's all. Supper will be ready in a few minutes. Meanwhile, we have some good news for you."

"I could use some." Maggie lowered herself into the rocking chair facing the couch. "What is it?"

"It's about the house," Steve said, leaning forward and bracing his elbows on his knees. "You have a buyer."

"Really?" Her face lit up instantly. "Who? When did this happen?"

"Right now," Steve said, and she could hear the pride in her son-in-law's voice. "It's April and me."

Maggie's face fell and she shot up out of her chair. "I should have known." Shaking her head, she started toward her room. "Forget it, guys. I'm not prepared to offer a big discount, I'm not going to offer owner financing so you can afford it, and I'm not going to rent it out to you. I need the equity out of it to live on, and—"

"Mags, just listen!" Steve stood up to stop her, then gestured for her to sit back down. "This is legit, I swear."

"We want to buy it like any other buyer," April said as Maggie folded her arms and stood stiffly in the doorway. "We're going to get a loan, and Steve's parents have offered us the money for a down payment, since they're so happy to see us getting on our own feet."

"And we're prepared to pay the price you came down to for that couple the other day," he said. "It's not the asking price, but it's only a couple thousand less."

Maggie frowned at them, but didn't make any move to sit down. "So I wouldn't have to do anything? Just sell it outright, get my money and move out?"

"That's all," Steve said. "My dad has connections at the mortgage company where his house is financed, and he thinks he can help us get the loan. We're both working now, and the day-care has been bringing in pretty good profits. There's no reason we'd be turned down."

"And we wouldn't have to disrupt our business, and you wouldn't have to completely say goodbye to the home you've had for the last eighteen years," April said. "Wouldn't you rather have us live here than strangers?"

"Well ... yes," Maggie said, still doubtful. "But you're sure this wouldn't cost me anything? I'd be able to move out free and clear?"

"The loan should take about six weeks to be approved," Steve said. "You'd have that long to find a place and get out. You could go sooner, though, if you wanted."

Maggie released the breath she'd been holding and allowed the proposal to sink in. Tiny measures of relief began to filter through her. "This really isn't a joke? You've looked into it and talked to people?"

"Yes, of course, we have," April said.

"And you've *asked* Steve's dad? You're not just making assumptions that he'll help you?"

"He volunteered it," Steve said. "He'd do anything to make sure we don't move back in with them."

A smile stole across Maggie's lips. "Wow. I can't believe this. Things do have a way of working out, don't they?"

"See, Mom? All you had to do was give Steve a little credit. I knew he could work this all out."

Maggie gave her son-in-law a long, scrutinizing look. "He sure did. Steve, I think you might turn out all right, after all."

"You better believe it," Steve said. "And we have plans for expanding. We're hiring a couple of new workers, and we'll be taking some preschool-education classes at night at the college next semester. And with the new workers, we'll be able to take a few more children—"

"Do me a favor," Maggie said, stemming his rambling with an upheld hand. "Wait till I'm gone to start all that, okay?"

"You got it," Steve said, "as long as you don't hang around indefinitely. We've got a business to run, you know."

Maggie breathed a disbelieving laugh as she headed for her bedroom.

Alone with the news she'd just heard slowly sinking in, Maggie's first thought was to call Jake and tell him. But that would be silly, she thought, when she'd spent all of her energy fighting her thoughts about him in the past few weeks. There really wasn't anyone else she cared to tell. Even though April and Steve's plans were just what she wanted to hear, they did nothing to lift the heaviness in her soul.

She picked up the box that had been delivered earlier, and sat down on the bed. She wondered if it was, indeed, safe to assume there was light at the end of her tunnel, or was this just another train coming to run her down?

Absently she opened the box, pulled out the object inside that was wrapped carefully in tissue and foam rubber. She caught her breath as she uncovered the tiny but intricately made sand castle, sparkling like a dream. There was no card, but she knew instantly who it was from.

She held the object in her hand for what seemed an eternity, staring at it and pondering its significance. Was Jake trying to remind her that some dreams did stay together? That all it took was a little tenderness? A little patience?

But that was why they were so different, she thought. Jake believed in sand castles. She believed in the strong winds that came and blew them down.

But she wanted to believe more.

Placing the sculpture onto the bed, she dropped her face into her hands as tears pushed to her eyes. Outside the door, she heard the telephone ring.

After a moment, April came to her door, knocked softly and opened it. "Mom? It's Jake again."

"I told you what to tell him," Maggie said, quickly wiping her tears. There was nothing more distressing than sharing her heartache over a man with her daughter. It was supposed to be the other way around.

"Mom, he's been really persistent. I almost feel sorry for him."

"Why?" Maggie asked. "You don't even like him."

"Not like him? How could I not like him? He delivered my baby. We named him after him. I think Jake's a great guy."

"Just as long as he isn't attached to me, right?" Maggie asked.

April joined Maggie on the bed, and putting her arm around her, said, "Mom, I know I was hard on you, but now I see how good Jake was for you. Don't avoid him just because of how embarrassed the two of you make me. I'm getting over it.''

"Gee, thanks," Maggie said, reaching for a tissue on her bed table. She had gone through at least a case of tissues lately. Fleetingly, she made a mental note to buy stock in the company that made them.

April made no move to go back to the phone. Quietly, she remained next to her mother. After a moment, she noticed the castle on the bed next to Maggie. "What's this?"

"A sand castle," Maggie replied, picking it up. "Someone sent it to me today."

"Jake?"

"Probably."

April studied the tiny structure, admiring it carefully. "He's really good, isn't he? There's a lot of heart in this."

"There's a lot of heart in Jake, period."

April moved her gaze back to her mother's tear-stained eyes. "Then why don't you take his call?"

"Because I can't," Maggie said. "It's over. It's better to get it all over with now than to keep anticipating what's inevitable."

"But don't you miss him at all?"

Maggie gave a tearful laugh and brought the sand castle to her heart. "Yeah, I miss him. You just wouldn't believe how—" She caught herself and stopped, realizing she hadn't meant to reveal that much. "Tell him I can't talk to him."

"No, Mom," April said. "I'll tell him you *won't*."

Her heart feeling bruised and wounded, Maggie watched as April left the room.

"WANT A LITTLE ADVICE?" April asked Jake when she came back to the phone after a good ten minutes, only to tell him that her mother wouldn't talk to him.

Jake frowned. "What?"

"Make her think you need her. Like you're dying or something. Tell her you're sick and that you can't get out of bed. She'll be over in two seconds flat."

"I don't want to play games, April," he said. "Your mother doesn't need anyone else manipulating her."

"Is that supposed to be a jab at me?" April asked. "Because I'll have you know that things are under control here. Steve and I are buying the house, and as soon as our loan goes through, Mom's getting an apartment and quitting her job so she can concentrate all her energies on school."

"Really? Can you and Steve swing that?"

"It's all in the works," April boasted. "Piece of cake."

"Well, that's great, April. That solves a lot of Maggie's problems."

"Not all of them, though. She still hasn't gotten over you, as tough as she is about talking to you. Jake, the bottom line is, if you want her back, you'll have to trick her. She's very stubborn."

After he had hung up the phone, Jake stared out his back doors, at the ocean beating against the shore in an autumn display of power. The beach had been pretty vacant today. The temperature had dropped lower than usual for this time of year. Somehow the change of seasons made him want Maggie more.

He wanted to see the end and beginning of every season with her. He wanted to see many, many more of them.

And April seemed to think that Maggie wanted that, too. So, damn it, what was she waiting for?

He got up and pulled on his jacket, zipped it up and went out across the deck and down the steps to the stretch of sand where he and Maggie had made love for the first time. She had been so warm against him, so sweet and trusting, so pliable, so responsive. It was the first time she'd told him her age and the first time he'd been able to show her that her age didn't matter.

As he looked out over the ocean, watching the froth on the tips of the waves and the sea gulls soaring on the blustering wind, something hit him that he had never felt before. The need for permanence. The need for stability. The need for a lifetime with Maggie.

It was something he'd never expressed to her, and only now did it occur to him that it was something she saw as an impossibility.

But what if he could show her that he wanted the same things she wanted? What if he could convince her that he could build her castles that wouldn't crumble? What if he could promise to not only help fulfill her dreams, but share in them?

Slowly he dropped onto his knees and began piling up the sand. With his artist's skill and patience he had cultivated over the years, he began to mold and shape the sand, getting more energetic as he went, for it had only now occurred to him that it was the answer he sought. The way to let Maggie know that he wasn't a bad risk. The way to let her see that he wouldn't take no for an answer.

Three hours later, he had finished his project, had covered it with candles and had lit it until the shapes glowed with a magical quality that couldn't be escaped. Smiling to himself, Jake went back to the telephone and decided that—manipulation or not—he was going to get Maggie over here somehow.

FROM HER DARK BEDROOM, Maggie heard the phone ring again, but she made no move to answer it. It stopped ringing and a moment later, her door opened and April stepped in. "Mom, are you awake? The phone's for you."

Maggie sat up, feeling miserably tired and empty, and looked at the phone on her bed table. "Who is it?"

"One of your professors, I think," April said. "Either that or one of your bosses. Somebody important."

Maggie frowned suspiciously at her daughter, but April backed out of the room and closed the door before she could drill her further. Cautiously she picked up the phone. "Hello?"

"Baggie, don't hang up."

It was Jake, only his voice didn't sound right, and something about the pleading in his tone cautioned her to hear him out. She would take care of April later, she thought.

"Jake, I really don't think—"

"Baggie, I deed your help. I'b burding with fever, and I can't breathe—"

Her heart jolted and she held the receiver tighter. "Jake, what's wrong? Are you sick?"

"I don't dow," he said. "I just didn't dow who else to call. Would you bind going to the drugstore for be? I really deed some flu medicine. Subthing to help be breathe."

All at once she recalled his coming to her house when she wasn't really even sick, with a bag full of cold medicine. It was the least—the very least—she could do for him. "Of course," she said, "I'll be right over."

"Baggie?"

"Yes?" she asked.

"I bight not be able to get up. If I don't answer the door, just cub on in."

"Okay," she said. "I'll be there as soon as I can."

Slamming the phone down, she grabbed the clothes she had slipped out of earlier, pulled them on and dashed out of her room. April was rocking Andy in the living room and called after her, "What's wrong?"

"It's Jake! He's sick."

Maggie didn't see the sly smile on April's face and Steve's wink as she ran past them on the way to her car.

JAKE'S HOUSE WAS DARK, and there was no answer when she knocked, so quietly, Maggie opened the door and stepped inside. "Jake?" she called.

There was no answer, so she dropped her purse onto the kitchen table and rushed into the bedroom. What if he'd passed out from fever? she thought on a wave of fear. What if something even worse had happened?

The bed was still made up, and there was no sign of Jake. Confused, she turned around in the doorway and scanned the living room. "Jake?"

Panic began to flood through her like a dangerous drug and she rushed to the studio, fearing with all her heart that she'd find him passed out on the floor. Oh, why hadn't she taken his call earlier today, when he wasn't as sick? Why hadn't she been here to fend off the fever and pamper him the way he would have pampered her had she really been sick on that first date?

She reached the studio and saw that it, too, was dark, except for one small lamp in the center of the room. Jake was nowhere to be seen. Maggie felt tears rising to her throat and the weight of her emotion pressing on her heart.

And then she saw what he had wanted her to see. Something that sat illuminated in that deliberate circle of light . . . a face, half-formed, half-unfinished, tilting its chin up in defiance of the world around it, smiling with hope and exhilaration, looking upward with fun in its eyes.

Her face.

Her fear melted away and she realized he had set her up so that she could see the vision he had of her. Instead of being angry, she was moved. As she drew closer, staring at the clay form, she realized that she hadn't looked like that in a very long time. The fun had died out of her eyes, and that youthful smile now felt old and strained.

"Jake?" she whispered as she bent over the sculpture and studied it more closely. The intricacies of her skin—every line and wrinkle, every flaw and every perfection, as well—were etched into the clay, and she knew he must have been working on it since they'd met. It would be a masterpiece without a doubt, she thought. And she had inspired it.

Joy filled her heart, and she wondered where he was and why he hadn't come out of hiding to gauge her reaction. "Jake, where are you?"

When there was still no answer, Maggie went back into the living room, expecting him to be there. There was still no sign of him.

That was when she saw the sliding glass doors to the deck were open. Slowly, she stepped outside.

Maggie caught her breath as she saw the flickering firelight on the beach behind Jake's house. Flames danced from six-foot-high letters that spelled out the most beautiful—and surprising—message she'd ever read.

Marry me, Maggie.

"Jake?" she cried to the night, and like a phantom, he emerged from the sand and the darkness.

Instantly his arms were around her, and as she threw hers around him, Maggie realized there was no place in her for logic and worry and dread. Only love and anticipation and joy filled her now, and she told herself that moments like this came once in a lifetime. The moments didn't last long, but they made lifetime memories.

And she'd made lots of lifetime memories with Jake.

"Will you, Maggie?" he asked, still crushing her in his embrace. "Will you marry me?"

"Oh, Jake," she cried as that old, familiar despair assaulted her again. "I can't marry you!"

"Why not?" he asked, his voice a warm rumble against her neck. "I love you. I know you love me, whether you'll admit it or not."

"But—"

"See there?" he whispered, not allowing her to pull away. "You didn't deny it. If it weren't true, you would have denied it right away."

Maggie pulled back enough to look at him. When he saw the tears in her eyes, he breathed out a soft moan and stroked the moisture from her cheeks. "How I feel doesn't matter, Jake. It's the other things."

"The grandparent thing?" he asked. "Maggie, I'm really looking forward to being a thirty-year-old grandfather. I won't have to change diapers, I won't have to get up at night, and if I get tired of him, I can give him back to his mother without any guilt. What could be better than that?"

She turned away, desperately struggling to sort through the confusing whirlwind of emotions, and looked at the message in the sand again. Quiet laughter edged up inside her, and she asked, "How did you do all that?"

"There you go, changing the subject." He came up behind her and slid his arms around her. "It took me hours and hours, Maggie. I wanted it to be the only proposal of its kind in the history of the world."

"Well, it is." She turned to him, slid her arms around his neck again and looked up at him. "And the clay sculpture in your studio... It's beautiful, Jake."

"That's because it's you."

"No," she said. "It's beautiful because of what you see in me. Something that hasn't been there in a long time."

"It isn't gone, Maggie. It just fell asleep from exhaustion. I want to help you wake it up again."

"You could, you know." The waves and wind played a synchronized piece, calming her troubled spirit, quieting her frightened soul as she gazed at him with glistening eyes.

"Marry me, Maggie," he whispered. "Please marry me. What better time is there? You're selling your house to the kids, and you're looking for a place to live anyway. I want you here with me. I want to share my bed with you. I want to share my whole life with you."

Maggie's tears came harder as the thought of such an arrangement struck her in the heart. It sounded wondrous, but it was too easy, too tempting. Long ago she had promised herself that if it meant being alone for the rest of her life, she'd never put herself through abandonment again. Could she risk it now, with so many things against them? "But what about your friends? Your family? What would they all think?"

"I can't help it if my friends would be green with envy that I got the most beautiful, sexiest, sweetest woman in the world to marry me. As for my family, they might decide that I've done something right for the first time in my life."

Maggie sucked in a sob and covered her mouth. "You've really thought this all out, haven't you?"

"Damn right, I have." The amusement faded from his face, and he touched her cheek softly as his eyes grew serious. "Darlin', without you, a big piece of me is missing. I need that piece, Maggie, and I don't ever want to face losing it again."

Her fear showed in her face. "Oh, Jake, I do love you. But I'm so scared. I never dreamed you would want to marry me. I thought—"

"That you were just a temporary plaything until I got tired of you? Maggie, this is serious business. The most serious business I've ever faced."

"But how can we be sure it wouldn't be a horrible mistake?"

"A mistake is something that backfires on you," he said, "and darlin', if you'll just say yes, I intend to spend the rest of my life protecting you from any more backfires."

For a moment, she stared up at him, tears rivering down her face in a warm display of the overflow of emotions she experienced in his arms. She had lived a long time already, but never before had she experienced such love from a man. It was a once-in-a-lifetime thing, she knew, and if she lost it now—if she threw it away—she'd never get that chance again.

Her voice was hoarse when she finally spoke. "Yes, Jake," she whispered. "Oh, yes."

He drew in a breath that sounded like a sob as he crushed her against him again. "From here on out, darlin', it's gonna be easy. It's gonna be heaven. You just wait and see."

Epilogue

Eight years later

Jake balanced the baby on one hip and angled the light just right on the sculpture he had been working on for the past ten months. It had turned out even better than he'd expected, and already several art critics were begging him for glimpses. The art journals were already saying that rumor had it his latest sculpture was "even better than the one entitled *Maggie Mine*," which had won three national awards several years ago and still sat on exhibit at the University Museum, to the chagrin of the New York art world, which had bargained to get it moved to a more prestigious place, until they realized he couldn't be budged.

But it was around this centerpiece that they were giving him his own exhibit in New York next month, and he'd spent the past few months preparing for it.

"What do you think, kiddo?" Jake asked the baby as he reached for the sculpture. Jake grabbed his hand and foiled his attempt to destroy it. "Yeah, I know, it isn't as pretty as the one of Grandma, but let's face it. Your grandma's a knockout."

"What are you telling him?"

Jake swung around and saw Maggie leaning in the doorway with laughter in her eyes, and he decided he was glad she'd heard. "Well, if it isn't Dr. Grandma," he said with a grin. "What are you doing home so early? Have you already cured all your clients?"

"No," she said. "But the Andersons have decided to get back together again, and I decided to give them a break from counseling this week while they take their second honeymoon. So I got to come home a little early. What are you doing with Ryan? Where's April?"

"Out back on the beach with Andy. He's building 'the biggest and best sand castle ever.' 'Course, we didn't have the heart to tell him it's already been done, did we, Ryan?" Ryan didn't answer as he seemed to be concentrating on something more important.

"Oh, no," Jake said. "Something died in Ryan's diaper."

Automatically, Maggie reached out to take him. "Come here, sport. Grandma'll change you."

"Oh, no, she won't," Jake said, holding the baby out of her reach.

Maggie laughed. "Well, don't tell me you plan to change him. The man who wants legislation to make it illegal for grandfathers to change diapers?"

"Ryan and I have the same understanding that Andy and I had," Jake said. "I don't change him and he won't change me. We're going to let his mother do it. Call her in."

Smiling, Maggie went to the back door and looked out to where April and Andy sat on the beach. It was unbelievable how big her first grandson had gotten. Already he was in the third grade, and she had to admit that April and Steve had done a terrific job with him.

The truth was, they had done a good job with a lot of things. They had actually made a success of Grandma's House, and had even opened a second location on the other side of town. Unbelievably, Steve had turned out to be a responsible and capable manager, and had even stopped wearing that earring.

Maggie called for April, and her daughter got up instantly and trod up the sand.

"Ryan needs changing," Maggie said, "and this is the kind of diaper only a mother could love."

"Gee, thanks," April said. "It's time for us to go home, anyway. It's getting to be time for his nap."

She took Ryan from Jake and disappeared into the bedroom.

Maggie turned back to Jake, who sat on the edge of a stool, grinning at her with that sexy grin that always made her tingle.

"Come here, you," he whispered.

She went willingly into his arms, letting him encompass her in the unconditional love and utter delight that he still seemed to have in her.

"What do you want, Grandpa?"

"I want to peel the clothes off of Grandma piece by piece and roll around in bed with her for the rest of the afternoon," he rumbled. "Any chance of that happening?"

She laughed. "April said she was just about to leave."

"Good," he whispered. He pulled her into a kiss, long and seductive and arousing, and when April stepped through the doorway, her moan did nothing to break the mood.

"Are you two at it again? Good grief. You'd think you were both teenagers."

As April left the house with Andy and Ryan, Maggie smiled up at her husband. "Are we alone?"

"No one else on the face of the Earth," Jake teased.

"Then what are we waiting for?"

They exchanged looks for a second, then simultaneously took off running toward the bedroom. Maggie shed her shoes and peeled off her panty hose as she ran, and Jake stepped out of his shorts and kicked them across the room. Her shirt was discarded somewhere in the living room, and her bra landed not far from it. Jake hurled his T-shirt into the bedroom, and it landed on the dresser.

No longer did Maggie feel self-conscious as she stood before Jake in the broad daylight pouring in through the window. Long ago he had convinced her that he cherished every inch of her body. To him, she was sexiness incarnate, youth personified, joy bottled like a drug that only he could enjoy.

And no matter how famous his work made him—or how successful she became—to her he would always be her Sand Man, holding her castles together with the magic of his infinite love.

ABOUT THE AUTHOR

Tracy Hughes began writing her first romance novel after graduating from Northeast Louisiana University in 1981. While in graduate school, she finished that book in lieu of her thesis, and decided to abandon her pursuit of a master's degree and follow her dream of becoming a writer. She is the award-winning author of over a score of novels, including a mainstream and a historical romance. Tracy makes her home in Mississippi with her two young daughters.

Books by Tracy Hughes
HARLEQUIN AMERICAN ROMANCE
381—HONORBOUND
410—SECOND CHANCES
438—FATHER KNOWS BEST

HARLEQUIN SUPERROMANCE
304—ABOVE THE CLOUDS
342—JO: CALLOWAY CORNERS, BOOK 2
381—EMERALD WINDOWS
399—WHITE LIES AND ALIBIS

Don't miss any of our special offers. Write to us at the following address for information on our newest releases.

Harlequin Reader Service
P.O. Box 1397, Buffalo, NY 14240
Canadian address: P.O. Box 603,
Fort Erie, Ont. L2A 5X3

THB10

WELCOME TO

The quintessential small town, where everyone
knows everybody else!

Finally, books that capture the pleasure
of tuning in to your favorite TV show!

Join your friends at Tyler in the eighth book, BACHELOR'S PUZZLE by Ginger
Chambers, available in October.

*What do Tyler's librarian and a cosmopolitan architect have in common? What
does the coroner's office have to reveal?*

GREAT READING…GREAT SAVINGS…
AND A FABULOUS FREE GIFT!

Each book set in Tyler is a self-contained love story; together, the twelve novels
stitch the fabric of the community. You can't miss the Tyler books on the shelves
because the covers honor the old American tradition of quilting; each cover
depicts a patch of the large Tyler quilt!

And you can receive a FABULOUS GIFT, ABSOLUTELY FREE, by collecting
proofs-of-purchase found in each Tyler book, *and* use our Tyler coupons to save
on your next TYLER book purchase.

Take 4 bestselling love stories FREE

Plus get a FREE surprise gift!

HARLEQUIN®

I N T R I G U E®

A SPAULDING AND DARIEN MYSTERY

Amateur sleuths Jenny Spaulding and Peter Darien have set
the date for their wedding. But before they walk down the
aisle, love must pass a final test. This time, they won't have to
solve a murder, they'll have to prevent one—Jenny's.
Don't miss the chilling conclusion to the SPAULDING AND
DARIEN MYSTERY series in October. Watch for:

#197 WHEN SHE WAS BAD by Robin Francis

Look for the identifying series flash—A SPAULDING AND
DARIEN MYSTERY—and join Jenny and Peter for danger and
romance....

If you missed the first three books in this four-book SPAULDING AND DARIEN MYSTERY series, #147 *Button, Button*, #159 *Double Dare*, or #171 *All Fall Down*, and would like to order
them, send your name, address, zip or postal code, along with a check or money order (please
do not send cash) for $2.50 for book #147, $2.75 for book #159, or $2.79 for book #171,
plus 75¢ postage and handling ($1.00 in Canada), payable to Harlequin Reader Service to:

In the U.S.
3010 Walden Avenue
P.O. Box 1325
Buffalo, NY 14269-1325

In Canada
P.O. Box 609
Fort Erie, Ontario
L2A 5X3

Please specify book title(s) with your order.
Canadian residents add applicable federal and provincial taxes.

SAD92R

HARLEQUIN®
AMERICAN ◆ ROMANCE®

American Romance's yearlong celebration continues.... Join your favorite authors as they celebrate love set against the special times each month throughout 1992.

Next month... Spooky things were expected in Salem, Massachusetts, on Halloween. But when a tall, dark and gorgeous man emerged from the mist, Holly Bennett thought that was going too far. Was he a real man...or a warlock? Find out in:

OCTOBER

S	M	T	W	T	F	S
				1	2	3
4					9	10
11	12		15	16	17
18	19				23	24
25	26	27	28	29	30	31

**#457
UNDER HIS SPELL
by Linda Randall Wisdom**

Read all the *Calendar of Romance* titles, coming to you one per month, all year, only in American Romance.

If you missed any of the *Calendar of Romance* titles—#421 *Happy New Year, Darling*; #425 *Valentine Hearts and Flowers*; #429 *Flannery's Rainbow*; #433 *A Man for Easter*; #437 *Cinderella Mom*; #441 *Daddy's Girl*; #445 *Home Free*; #449 *Opposing Camps*; or #455 *Sand Man*—and would like to order them, send your name, address, zip or postal code, along with a check or money order for $3.29 each for #421 and #425 or $3.39 each for #429, #433, #437, #441, #445, #449, or #455, plus 75¢ postage and handling ($1.00 in Canada) *for each book ordered*, payable to Harlequin Reader Service to:

In the U.S.
3010 Walden Avenue
P.O. Box 1325
Buffalo, NY 14269-1325

In Canada
P.O. Box 609
Fort Erie, Ontario
L2A 5X3

Please specify book title(s) with your order.
Canadian residents add applicable federal and provincial taxes.

COR10